ANOTHER MOMENT IN TIME

Another Collection of Short Stories

SUSAN STOKER

Four stories by Susan Stoker, including Caroline's Surprise, Carnal Comfort, Best Christmas Ever, and First Kiss.

Caroline's Surprise- Caroline thinks her husband, Matthew "Wolf" Steel, is taking her out to dinner for their twenty-fifth anniversary, but he's got a bigger surprise in store.

Carnal Comfort - When Trigger finds his girlfriend having a nightmare on their couch, he's surprised and unhappy she left their bed to suffer alone. But when he asks what he can do to help, he's even more surprised by the answer.

Best Christmas Ever- When Chris and Sienna meet during an accident in Texas, the perfect strangers soon discover they're inexplicably linked...in more ways than one. Coincidence? Perhaps. Or maybe the makings of their very own Christmas miracle.

First Kiss- Annie Fletcher is far more tomboy than girly-girl; Frankie Sanders has a disability most boys don't have to endure. But in each other's eyes, they're perfect—and the teen sweethearts have waited nearly a decade for their first kiss.

If they can find more than a few minutes alone

during his holiday visit, Frankie and Annie's Christmas promises to be the most magical ever.

<u>To sign up for Susan's Newsletter go to</u>: http://www.stokeraces.com/contact-1.html

CAROLINE'S SURPRISE

by Susan Stoker

NOTE FROM THE AUTHOR

Caroline's surprise was originally featured in an anthology (that is no longer available) to raise money for Australia to fight the wildfires that ravaged that country in 2019/2020.

This story comes *before* The Boardwalk (included in *A Moment in Time- A Collection of Short Stories*) and if you've read that story, you know that Caroline's 25th anniversary is one of her treasured memories.

I wanted to write that story, that memory. No tears with this story, promise. :)

If you want the full effect of Caroline and Wolf's story from the beginning, the order to read the books is:

Protecting Caroline
Marrying Caroline
Caroline's Surprise
The Boardwalk

Enjoy!
-Susan

BLURB FOR CAROLINE'S SURPRISE

Caroline thinks her husband, Matthew "Wolf" Steel, is taking her out to dinner for their twenty-fifth anniversary, but he's got a bigger surprise in store.

CAROLINE'S SURPRISE

CAROLINE STEEL SIGHED in exasperation as she looked at her husband. She and Matthew "Wolf" Steel had been married for twenty-five years. Today was their anniversary, in fact. They'd checked into a fancy hotel by a beach near their Southern California home, and she'd been looking forward to dinner at one of the finest steakhouses the city had to offer.

But her *dear* husband had just informed her that he wanted to take a walk on the beach before they ate.

"This dress you bought me yesterday isn't exactly appropriate for a beach walk," Caroline protested.

"You look beautiful," Matthew told her.

Caroline loved when he complimented her, but at the moment, she was too irritated to appreciate his comment. "These shoes are going to be impossible on the beach," she told him, trying to think of another excuse that would get her out of his crazy idea.

Her husband loved the ocean. Loved everything about it. The way the wind blew on the coast, the smell of the water, the salt in the air that you could actually taste on your lips. Normally, Caroline did too, but she'd just spent an hour doing her hair and makeup, wanting it to be perfect for their dinner. They'd gone shopping yesterday, and Matthew had bought her the most beautiful floor-length pink dress. It had little cap sleeves and flared out from her waist, making her feel like a princess.

At fifty-seven, Caroline knew she was too old to be considered pretty. The fact of the matter was, she'd *never* been a beauty. She was plain. Boring. But Matthew had always said that, from almost the second he'd seen her, he'd known she was the woman for him. They'd met in an unconventional way, on a plane that had been hijacked by terrorists. Because of her background as a chemist, Caroline had been able to help save everyone on board. But then the people behind the hijacking had come after her...

She didn't like to dwell on that time in her life, but it had brought her Matthew, so she didn't regret one second of what had happened.

Matthew was sixty-one, and instead of looking like a wrinkled old man, he seemed to get more distinguished with age. His hair was sprinkled with a healthy dose of gray, but he kept it cut short, just as he had when he was a Navy SEAL. He'd lost the bulk of the muscles he'd had as a younger man, but Caroline was still just as attracted to him today as she'd been twenty-five years ago when they'd gotten married.

There had been some hiccups on their wedding day—namely, they'd never made it to the church because of a car accident involving their friends—but that hadn't stopped them. They'd ended up saying their vows in the emergency room, surrounded by all their loved ones. Caroline had never regretted not having a traditional wedding; she was too thankful to have Wolf as her very own.

But, there were times when her husband drove her crazy. Like now.

He had no idea what walking along the boardwalk would do to her hair. It would blow all her hard work to smithereens. By the time they arrived at the restaurant, she'd look pathetic, and Matthew would probably look just as polished and handsome as he did right this minute.

He was wearing a pair of jeans and a navy polo. And while some people might think it odd that he was wearing denim to a fancy restaurant, Caroline loved that he did what he wanted, wore what he wanted, and could get away with it.

"Matthew, seriously, I want to look good for you tonight, and if we walk along the ocean, I'm going to be a mess."

Matthew walked toward her and took her head in his hands. Tilting it up so she had to look in his eyes, he said lovingly, "You always look beautiful, Ice. I don't care if you wear your pajamas or this beautiful dress. You're the love of my life, and I'm always proud to be by your side."

She shivered in delight when he called her Ice. He'd given her the nickname back when they'd first met, and it always made her go gooey inside when he uttered it. "Matthew," Caroline complained, "I love you, but sometimes you're clueless."

"Just for a little bit," Matthew cajoled. "We won't stay long, but I have it on good authority that there's something you're going to want to see on the beach this evening."

Caroline sighed, knowing when she was beaten. When Matthew's voice got low and he gave her those puppy dog eyes, she couldn't deny him anything. "Fine, but if we're late for our reservations, I'm blaming you."

Her husband beamed. "Deal." Then he leaned down

and kissed her. The kiss started out tender and light, but soon morphed into something much more passionate. They might be older and not have the stamina they used to, but their sex life was still active and intense.

Caroline pulled back and put her hand on her husband's cheek. "I love you," she told him.

"I love you too. And I plan on showing you how much tonight when we get back here to our room."

"I can't believe you got the honeymoon suite," Caroline said with a shake of her head. "I would've been perfectly happy with a regular room. This one is way too expensive."

"Nothing is too expensive for you," Matthew said. "I might not be able to buy you a brand-new Lamborghini, but I can splurge every now and then on a nice hotel room with some extras to make sure you know how much you're loved."

"Like the dozen roses?" Caroline asked, peeking over at the gorgeous bouquet on the table next to the bed. She'd wanted them as close to her as possible so she could smell them all night, even while she was sleeping.

"And the chocolate-covered strawberries, and the champagne," Matthew said with a smile. "Now, come on, we need to get going," he told her, grabbing hold of her hand and pulling her toward the door.

"I swear, if there's a volleyball tournament with

scantily clad women jumping around, I'm gonna have to hurt you," Caroline mock threatened.

"Maybe they're guys wearing banana hammocks," Matthew teased.

"Ewwww. Gross," Caroline said on a laugh. She adored that her husband still made her laugh after all these years. When they were on the elevator on the way to the lobby, Caroline leaned into Wolf. "If I forget to tell you later, thank you for the best twenty-five years of my life."

He kissed the top of her head. "I think that's my line."

The doors opened, and Matthew exited slightly in front of Caroline. It was one of the small ways he was always protecting her. Always on the lookout for people walking too fast who could run into her, or ruffians who might think they were an easy mark because of their ages. Matthew had surprised more than one person with his strength and determination to keep her safe.

They walked through the lobby, and Matthew nodded at the concierge as he passed. Then they were on the street walking toward the boardwalk nearby. It wasn't much of a boardwalk, really, more like an old wooden walkway along a stretch of sand. It wasn't very long, but Caroline liked the benches the city had placed along the route, and the fact there were people out and about, from young to old, enjoying the fresh ocean air.

She and Matthew walked hand in hand, and Caroline had to admit that this was a great idea. Her husband held her shoes in his left hand and held on to her tightly with his right. "I can't decide which beach is my favorite," she said easily. "I mean, I love Southern California, and we've spent most of our time here, but there was something so magical about the beach in Alaska."

"Magical?" Matthew asked. "It was damn cold if you asked me."

Caroline laughed. "Well, at least you didn't have to swim in it."

"Not *that* time, I didn't," he retorted.

Caroline didn't know all the details about the missions her husband had gone on as a SEAL, but she knew that's what he was referring to. She squeezed his hand, trying to let him know how proud she was of him, then went on with her thought. "The boardwalk in New Jersey was fun. All the stalls with food and arcade games. I liked that beach too."

Matthew grunted. She knew that hadn't been his favorite vacation, but he'd gone because she'd wanted to experience it.

"I think Hawaii was my second favorite," she went on. "Not Waikiki, there were too many people there to truly enjoy the beaches, but the North Shore was amazing. I can't believe how big those waves were. The surfers were insane! But there's one beach I keep hearing about that I'd love to visit."

"Where's that? I'll get a ticket tomorrow," Matthew said.

And Caroline knew he wasn't kidding. He would totally go online and buy them tickets to wherever she wanted to go. Leaning against him, she wrapped her arm around his waist, enjoying the feel of his own around her shoulders. They kept walking down the boardwalk at a slow and steady pace. People easily passed them, walking, running, biking, and riding scooters, but neither seemed to notice.

"Australia. I've never been there, but everyone I've talked to who's visited has said the people are lovely. I even went and looked up famous beaches over there."

"You want to go to the Great Barrier Reef?" Wolf asked.

Caroline shook her head. "No. I mean, yes, I'd love to see it, but I think I'd like to visit Bondi Beach. It's only about thirty minutes from downtown Sydney, and there are a ton of great restaurants in the area. The history of it is fascinating. Bondi was origi-nally Boondi, which is an aboriginal word meaning 'surf' in English. It's iconic, and I'd love to see it someday."

Matthew stopped abruptly in the middle of the boardwalk, and Caroline looked up at him. "What's wrong?"

"Nothing's wrong. If you want to go to Australia, I'll take you to Australia. I'll make sure you see kangaroos, koalas, and echidnas. We'll go to a show at the famous opera house and have dinner with the Sydney bridge in the background. And yes, we'll go to Bondi Beach. I'll even swallow my pride and take you to Manly Beach."

Caroline giggled. "Is that really what it's called?"

"Yup. But don't get your hopes up, the only man I want you ogling at Manly Beach is me."

"That's a given," Caroline said, snuggling up to her husband. "And thank you for indulging me."

"I'd do anything for you," Matthew said. "Come on, the thing I wanted to show you is just ahead."

Caroline had already forgotten that Matthew wanted to show her something. She assumed it was maybe a sandcastle building contest or something. She'd always been fascinated with the detailed sand creations people could make.

They walked farther down the beach until Caroline saw a large group of people gathered on the sand ahead of them. She couldn't see what was going on, but figured that was where Matthew was taking her.

Caroline wasn't paying attention to where they were going, too busy daydreaming about Australia and holding a cute koala bear, when Matthew stopped and turned toward the beach.

She finally focused—and gasped in surprise.

She *knew* the people on the beach. They were their friends.

All of Matthew's SEAL teammates were there with their wives. Abe and Alabama, Cookie and Fiona, Mozart and Summer, Dude and Cheyenne, Benny and Jessyka, and his old commander with his wife, Julie, too. Even Tex and Melody were there.

Not only that, but many of the other SEAL men they'd gotten to know over the years were also there with *their* wives. Children were everywhere, the older ones looking after the younger ones.

And every single person was wearing white. White shirts, dresses, pants. It was as if a cloud of white had descended on the beach...and it was beyond beautiful.

There were also rows of chairs set up in the sand facing what looked like an altar.

"What? What's happening?" Caroline asked, looking up at Matthew.

"I'd go down on one knee, but we both know I'd

probably make an ass out of myself trying to get up since my knees are shot. I'm sorry you missed out on your beautiful church wedding twenty-five years ago, Ice. I thought you might like a do-over of sorts, and we could renew our vows right here."

"*Now?*" she asked stupidly.

Matthew grinned. "Yeah. Right now. All our friends are here. I'm sorry, but I lied about dinner at that fancy steak place. I promise to take you there later. The hotel here"—he gestured to a large hotel behind them—"is catering a reception right on the beach after our ceremony."

Caroline wanted to cry. Matthew wasn't the most traditionally romantic man. The roses and chocolates back in their honeymoon suite were the most traditional things he'd done in a very long time. But he showed her every day how much he loved and cared about her. Filled up her car with gas, made dinner most nights for them, took the garbage out, held her hand everywhere they went. She'd always take Wolf exactly the way he was, without the over-the-top romantic gestures.

But this...this was the most amazing thing that had ever happened to her. She knew how much work went into planning something like this. From talking to the hotel to getting all their friends to coordinate their schedules. "Was this what you were doing all those times I caught you being all secret-like?"

He looked a bit sheepish. "Yes. I prayed you wouldn't think I was cheating on you or something. All those late-night phone calls and the extra time I was spending on the computer. I just wanted this night to be perfect for you. I'd give you the moon if I could swing it."

"I love you, Matthew. So much."

"And I love you too. So? What do ya think? Shall we do this?"

"Yes!" Caroline exclaimed.

They walked hand in hand toward their friends, and Caroline noticed that Matthew had even hired a professional photographer who was clicking away on his camera as they approached the group.

As soon as they got close, they were surrounded by their friends. Everyone wanted to give their congratulations and crow about how they'd been able to keep this a secret from her.

Caroline accepted their teasing and knew she was smiling like an idiot. She had no idea where Matthew had put her shoes, and was well aware that her hair—which she'd worked so painstakingly to put up—was blowing out of control, but she no longer cared one bit.

After fifteen minutes of saying hello to everyone

and thanking them for coming, Matthew whistled sharply. "Okay everyone, enough chitchat. Time for me to marry my wife...again."

Everyone laughed. It took a few minutes to wrangle the children, but soon everyone was sitting and gazing back expectantly at Caroline and Matthew at the end of the makeshift aisle in the sand.

"You ready?" Matthew whispered.

"For you? Always," Caroline told him.

Then they walked slowly down the aisle toward the justice of the peace Matthew had hired. Caroline barely held it together as he welcomed everyone. He spoke of everlasting love and friendship. His words were heartfelt and resonated within Caroline.

She and Matthew gazed into each other's eyes while he was talking, and she'd never felt closer to her husband.

Soon, it was Matthew's turn to speak.

Caroline blinked in surprise and realized that she was going to have to come up with something romantic and witty to say on the spur of the moment. She wasn't ready! Had no idea what to say.

But then...she couldn't think about *anything* but Matthew's words.

"Twenty-five years ago, I took you as my wife. I thought it was the best day of my life, but I was wrong. Every day that followed was the best day. I believe in our marriage, in us, more strongly today than ever before. You never wavered in your support of me. Every time I said goodbye and went on a mission for the Navy, you never showed your fear. Never did or said anything to let me know you were feeling anything other than support and love for me.

"But I know you were scared. Terrified that you wouldn't see me again. You did what you needed to do, and that made our reunions all the more sweet. I love you, Caroline Steel. You've made me a better man in every single way. I stand here in front of you today, with our friends as witnesses, to renew my original vows to you. Through sickness and health. I will protect you, stand by you—and in front of you, if needed. I will put you first, because you spent much of our marriage putting my wants and needs ahead of your own. No matter where life takes us in the next twenty-five years, know that I will always be there for you."

Caroline was crying ugly tears. The kind that made her eyes red and puffy, but she couldn't help it. She never would've thought she could be as happy as she was right this second—and Matthew had kept her pretty damn happy the last twenty-five years. When she'd first met him, she'd been at a weird place in her life. Wanting to find someone who would appreciate her for who she was, but not thinking it would ever happen. She'd been overlooked by just about everyone. But after a rocky start, Matthew had *seen* her. And had loved her anyway.

"Your turn, Ice," Matthew said with a small smile. He reached out and wiped the tears off her cheeks gently, then tucked a lock of hair behind her ear.

"I'm not sure I can follow that," Caroline said honestly. "But I'll try. There *were* times over the last twenty-five years when I wasn't sure I could do this. Be married to a Navy SEAL. To a man larger than life like you. I was afraid I'd fade into the background and be lost in your shadow. But from day one of our marriage, you refused to let that happen. Through your strength and love, I blossomed. You gave me the gift of friendship with your teammates, and I gained sisters through their wives.

"I love you more today because of all that we've been through. I promise to be by your side when you're sick, hurt, or in need of comfort. I promise to make sure you know how appreciated you are every day for the rest of our lives, no matter how long that might be. I'm not scared to live to be a hundred and ten, because I know you'll be by my side, loving me, protecting me, and giving me the best life you can. I love you, Matthew. I can't wait to see what the next twenty-five years has in store for us."

"I love you," Matthew whispered as he leaned close.

"I think you're supposed to wait to be told to kiss her!" Dude yelled from the audience, but Matthew ignored him.

Caroline grinned before her husband kissed her as passionately as he had the first time they'd gotten married. It might make some of the younger kids on the beach wince, but she couldn't wait to get Matthew back to their honeymoon suite and show him how much he meant to her.

As if he could read her mind, Matthew whispered against her lips, "Reception first, Ice, then bed." He pulled back, turned her to face their audience, and held up their clasped hands. "Married...again!" he yelled.

Caroline knew she was smiling crazily but didn't care in the least. When Matthew was happy, she was happy.

Once again, they were surrounded by their friends, everyone congratulating them and telling them how beautiful the ceremony was.

They all walked up to the hotel as a group, and Caroline gasped at the setup. It was both elegant and laid-back...which fit the setting perfectly. There were beautiful flower arrangements on every table with candles she knew would give the area a romantic glow after the sun went down. The tables were placed right in the sand, and a huge buffet was arranged off to the side.

Matthew led her to the front of the line and proceeded to pile her plate high with food.

"Matthew, I can't eat all that!" Caroline protested, laughing.

"You can try," he told her.

"Why are you always trying to get me to eat?" she grumbled as he led the way to one of the tables.

"Because you need the vitamins," he said with a smile. "Gotta get the proper nutrients in you when I can. If it was left up to you, you'd eat nothing but doughnuts and other junk food."

Caroline smiled because he was probably right.

"And before you complain, green beans are good for you," Matthew told her. "And...you know I'll eat what you can't finish."

She *did* know that. Matthew had been eating her leftovers for as long as they'd been married. It was kind of their thing. Of course, he wasn't a Navy SEAL anymore and had to watch how much he ate, but they both loved the tradition they'd started so long ago.

The meal was delicious, and Caroline didn't even mind the wind blowing her hair in her food or how the seagulls were standing watch only feet away, waiting for a child to leave their plate unattended, or the chance to snatch a dropped piece of bread.

When the staff brought out dessert, Caroline wasn't surprised to see what Matthew had chosen.

"German chocolate cake?" she asked with a laugh.

"Yup. It's our favorite."

"*Your* favorite," she corrected.

"Yup," he agreed again, not looking abashed in the least.

Caroline didn't mind. He deserved an extra-large slice of his all-time favorite cake for pulling off this surprise. Everything had been perfect as far as she was concerned. And she loved Matthew all the more for putting it together.

She ate as much as she could of her cake and grinned when Matthew pulled her unfinished portion over in front of him.

As he polished off the rest of her slice, Caroline rested her head on his shoulder. A waiter brought over a tea kettle filled with hot water and a bag of Earl Gray tea. She smiled at her husband.

"Now that's really *your* favorite," he said with confidence.

"It is," Caroline agreed. "You spoil me."

"I'd do anything for you," he told her.

After she'd finished her tea, Wolf stood and held out his hand to her. Caroline took it and he led her to the middle of all the tables, where there was a small space in the sand. He pulled out his phone and clicked on it a few times until the sound of their wedding song filled the air around them.

"May I have this dance?" Matthew asked.

Caroline nodded as he took her in his arms. They swayed back and forth in the sand as "Come To Me" by the Goo Goo Dolls played. It was an unconventional wedding song, but she'd never forget how he'd changed the lyrics twenty-five years ago to perfectly fit their situation and their courtship. She'd loved him then, and she loved him now. More than she could adequately put into words.

When they finished their dance, Caroline realized that most of their friends had stood up and were swaying back and forth as well. There was so much love around them, Caroline almost felt overwhelmed.

"The sun's about to set. Come with me," Matthew said, pulling her toward the ocean. Caroline went without a fuss.

Matthew stopped just beyond where the waves reached the sand on the beach and turned to face her. He put his arms around her waist, and she rested her palms on his chest.

"I'm sorry I lied to you," Matthew told her. "I really wanted this to be a surprise."

"You can lie to me about things like this all you

want," she replied, grinning. "No one other than you has ever made me feel so special and loved."

"You *are* loved," Matthew said seriously. "Everyone was thrilled to come today. We might not have had kids, but everyone here thinks of you as their second mother."

"I know. Remember that time I thought it would be a good idea to have thirteen of those little stinkers over at the same time so their parents could have some time alone?" she asked.

"Don't remind me," Matthew said, mock shuddering.

"Do you regret not having kids?" she couldn't help but ask.

"No." His answer was immediate and firm. "I've loved having you to myself. I know that makes me a selfish bastard, but there ya go. Besides, we've practically helped raise our friends' kids, I don't feel as if we've missed out."

"But we don't have anyone to take care of us when we get old."

"Some people would say we're *already* old," Matthew said without a hint of worry in his tone. "Besides, you've got *me* to take care of you, and you'll take care of me. We'll be fine."

Just then, Tex's granddaughter, his daughter Akilah's firstborn, crashed into Wolf's legs, almost knocking him over. She was only four but already quite smart. "Tag, Uncle Wolf, you're it!" the little girl yelled, then dashed away.

Matthew looked back up at Caroline and quirked his eyebrow. "Not have kids?" he asked dryly with a grin.

Caroline threw her head back and laughed until her stomach hurt. He was right. She may not have given birth to a child, but she'd definitely done her part in raising the young men and women who'd shared their special day. And now those kids were having their own children. The cycle of life would continue, and both she and Wolf had more than enough family to take care of them if they needed it when they were older.

"Look," Matthew said softly, turning her to watch the sun go down beyond the horizon.

Caroline was always surprised at how fast it happened. One second the sun was there as an orange ball in the sky, and the next it was just gone.

Life was like that. One day you were happy and living the best life you could, and the next you were gone. But never forgotten.

Everyone left a legacy behind, and she hoped she and Matthew would leave a good one.

As they made their way back up to the reception area, the photographer—who'd followed them without their knowledge—showed them a picture he'd taken. It was of the two of them standing by the ocean, the sun setting behind them. Caroline was laughing with her head thrown back, and Matthew was looking down at her, smiling.

"Oh my God," Caroline gasped as she looked at the picture on the man's camera. "I'm totally framing that."

The man smiled. "Yeah, I think it's my favorite of the night, and that's saying something, because you have a beautiful family."

Yes, they certainly did.

* * *

Later that night, Wolf slowly unzipped the beautiful pink dress and slipped it off Caroline's shoulders. He couldn't believe how beautiful his wife still was. She had more wrinkles than she used to, and she complained that her skin sagged in all the wrong places, but all he saw was perfection.

She went into the bathroom to get ready for bed, and he did the same in the second bathroom the luxury suite provided.

They met back in the bedroom, and Caroline climbed on the bed and opened her arms to him.

Wolf quickly joined her, pulling her into his embrace. He inhaled deeply, loving the smell of salt and the fresh ocean air that lingered on her skin.

Neither of them were young anymore, but that had never stopped them from loving each other. Wolf eased his way down Caroline's body, excited by the look in her half-closed eyes as he spread her legs and settled himself between them.

After he'd sent her soaring with an orgasm, he climbed back up her body and eased himself inside her. He made love to his wife slow and easy, never taking his eyes from hers. He didn't last long, never did anymore, but that didn't matter to either of them.

Closing his eyes and memorizing the feel of Caroline under and around him, Wolf exploded.

He gathered his wife into his arms again and covered them both with the sheet. She snuggled into him just as she had for the last twenty-five years.

"What's your favorite memory from our life together so far?" Caroline asked sleepily.

"You waking up next to me, and seeing the love in your eyes when you open them and see *me*," Wolf said without hesitation.

"Really?" Caroline asked. "Out of everything we've done, that's your favorite?"

"Absolutely," Wolf told her. "What about you?"

"It's impossible for me to narrow it down to one

thing," Caroline said with a small shake of her head. "It's the way you always make me feel as if what I say matters. The way you listen...really *listen* to me. When we look at each other, and it's like we're thinking the same thing, like we share a brain."

"I love that," Wolf admitted.

She was quiet for so long that Wolf thought she'd fallen asleep, but then she surprised him by saying quietly, "I think the reason I wake up looking at you with love in my eyes is because I always sleep well, knowing you're watching over me."

Wolf felt his eyes misting. He wasn't a crier. Never had been. Being a Navy SEAL had pretty much assured that. He'd seen and experienced too much to cry at the drop of a hat. But her words struck him hard.

"I'll *always* watch over you, Ice. No matter what happens in the future. You can count on me."

He'd expected a loving reply, but all he got was a light snore.

Chuckling softly, Wolf closed his eyes and tightened his grip on his wife. He and Caroline were a matched pair. And while he had no idea what was in store for him and Ice in the future, he knew without a doubt he'd do whatever it took to make the next half century just as great as the first twenty-five had been.

CARNAL COMFORT

by Susan Stoker

NOTE FROM THE AUTHOR

This short story was originally featured in an audio-only anthology. The Hero and heroine in this story were in *Shielding Gillian,* the first book in my Delta Team two series. and this story takes place *after* that one.

We all know trauma can come back and haunt us, even if we're happy. So the idea for Gillian's struggle to deal with nightmares was born. And of course her man, Trigger, is more than willing to help her deal with her bad memories, in a most satisfying way. :)

The story is super hot, as the audio was read by a popular male narrator...and I figured my female readers would appreciate that.

-Susan

BLURB FOR CARNAL COMFORT

When Trigger finds his girlfriend having a nightmare on their couch, he's surprised and unhappy she left their bed to suffer alone. But when he asks what he can do to help, he's even more surprised by the answer.

CARNAL COMFORT

TRIGGER ROLLED over and reached for Gillian. But his hand met only cold sheets next to him.

Sitting up, he was immediately awake.

Something had been up with Gillian lately, but she wasn't telling him what it was, no matter how he tried to convince her that she could open up with him, that she was safe telling him anything.

A noise from the other room had Trigger on his feet before he'd even thought about what he was doing. Wearing nothing but a pair of boxer shorts, he tiptoed silently out of the master bedroom and down the hall.

He and Gillian have moved into a three-bedroom house not too long ago, as his apartment had been way too small for them. Gillian and her best friends had been overjoyed to decorate. Trigger didn't give as shit about matching pillows or the giant watercolor painting of a longhorn steer they'd put in the living room. But he did love the pictures Gillian had framed and put on every available surface.

Pictures of the two of them. Pictures of Trigger with his best friends...and fellow Delta Force members. Pictures of Gillian with *her* friends. Everywhere he looked were memories that made him smile. Before meeting Gillian, he hadn't known what he was missing, and she showed him every day how lucky he was to have her in his life.

Checking each of the other bedrooms as he passed, Trigger saw they were empty. Whatever he'd heard hadn't come from either room. Then he heard what had woken him up again.

"Noooo!

It was Gillian's voice—and she sounded terrified.

His blood running cold, Trigger ran into the living room. He skidded to a halt when he didn't see an intruder holding the love of his life hostage.

What greeted him was worse.

Gillian was lying on the couch, a pillow under her head and one of the many fuzzy blankets she'd accumulated over the years over her body. She'd obviously left their bed to come out here to sleep, which gutted Trigger.

As he tried to come to terms with what he was

seeing, Gillian's head rolled back and forth on the pillow and her legs thrashed. "Stop! No!" she whined.

She was having a hell of a nightmare, and Trigger hated that they'd returned after all these months. He was at her side in a heartbeat.

"Gilly, wake up," he said in a low but firm tone.

"Run, Walker!" Gillian exclaimed frantically.

"You're having a nightmare, wake up," he tried again.

"Walker! Get away! They're going to kill you!"

Hating that he had to put his hands on her, but knowing he didn't have a choice—she wasn't coming out of the nightmare on her own—Trigger shook Gillian's shoulders roughly. He needed to get her awake, then they could deal with whatever it was she'd been dreaming about.

The second his hands landed on her, Gillian's eyes popped open and she screamed.

"It's me. Walker. You're okay, Gillian!" Trigger said urgently.

It took a second, but he breathed out a sigh of relief when recognition hit.

"Walker?"

"Yeah, Gilly, it's me."

She inhaled deeply, then threw herself into his arms. Trigger caught her, wrapping one arm around her back and the other curling around her nape, holding her tightly. Her breaths were short and choppy against the skin of his neck and he could feel her trembling.

Neither spoke for a long moment. Trigger wanted to give her some time to calm down, to know that she was safe.

"Sorry," she whispered after a while.

"No need to be sorry for having a nightmare," Trigger said, pulling back so he could see her eyes. "But I can't say I'm happy that you snuck out of our bed to sleep here."

Gillian's eyes dropped. "I didn't want to bother you."

"You're *never* a bother," Trigger said firmly.

"I am," Gillian countered. "Besides, you have to get up early tomorrow to work out with your team."

"*You* are more important than anything else," Trigger said. "Talk to me. Tell me what's going on."

Gillian sighed. "I'm just having a bad week."

Knowing she wasn't telling him everything, Trigger made a decision. He shifted his grip and stood with Gillian in his arms. She didn't cry out, didn't ask what he was doing, she simply snuggled into his chest as he moved to carry her down the hall and back to their bedroom. Placing her carefully on their bed, Trigger helped her get under the covers, then crawled in after her. He turned her so they were chest to chest, and he wrapped his arms around her once more.

Once they were both settled, he said, "What was the dream about?"

She stiffened for a second, but then seemed to melt into him.

"I was back on that hijacked plane in Venezuela. You were coming to save me, but I knew Luis and the other hijackers planned to kill you. They were going to ambush you. I tried to warn you, but you didn't hear me. Luis had a gun raised and was about ready to shoot you when I woke up."

Trigger hated that she was still having nightmares about the hijacking. "It was that crime TV producer, calling and asking questions for the show they're filming about what happened, wasn't it?" he asked.

Gillian nodded against his chest.

"For the record, I don't like waking up without you," Trigger told her. "I don't care how much you toss and turn, I'll always sleep better with you by my side. You suffering in silence out on the couch makes me feel like shit."

"I'm sorry," she told him.

"What do you need to feel better?" Trigger asked, willing to do anything. "We can watch a movie, or I can get you a book. If you want to listen to music or even work, that's okay too."

Gillian tilted her head back and looked at him for a long moment.

"What?" he asked, hating that he couldn't read what was on her mind.

"Anything?"

"Of course. Name it, and it's yours," Trigger told her.

"I need you to make love to me. I need to feel you inside me and know that it was only a dream and that you're here, alive and well."

Trigger's cock twitched. Gillian smiled, and he knew she could feel him harden against her belly. "Are you sure?"

"Positive," she said firmly.

Pushing her back so she was looking up him, Trigger's hands went to the bottom of the tank top she was wearing. He slowly drew it upward, loving how Gillian eagerly arched her back, helping him get it over her head.

Throwing the material to the side, not caring about where it landed, Trigger looked down at the woman he loved more than life. She was extremely strong. He'd never met anyone stronger. He'd nicknamed her Di, for Diana Prince, Wonder Woman's alter ego, because that's what she was to him. She'd more than proven her strength and leadership skills all those months ago when she'd been thrust into the role of negotiator on a hijacked plane. The longer Trigger was with her, the more in awe of her he became.

Gillian gave him a small smile and put her arms above her head, arching her back slightly and pushing her chest up toward him. Not being a stupid man, Trigger took the hint. He leaned down and covered one nipple with his lips, and pinched the other with his fingers.

He loved the sigh that left her lips at his touch. Trigger flicked the rapidly tightening bud with his tongue, and didn't let up with his teasing until her nipple was hard. He lightly nipped it, smiling when she shifted restlessly under him. His Gilly was extremely responsive, and there were days he still couldn't believe she was his.

He switched sides, taking her other nipple into his mouth as he squeezed and massaged her tits. When he felt her fingers clutch at the back of his head, he closed his eyes in pleasure. He loved her touch. Her hands were so much softer than his own and it just highlighted the differences between them.

He opened his eyes and slid down her body, pushing the sheet off them as he went, giving himself a clear view of her body. He took hold of the elastic of her panties, loving how Gillian eagerly lifted her hips, making it easy for Trigger to slide them down her legs.

It was ridiculous how pleased he was to see how wet Gillian was already. Knowing he could turn her on was a definite ego boost, although he had a feeling she'd tell him he didn't need a bigger ego. Smiling, Trigger lowered his head and nuzzled her inner thigh, prolonging the moment.

"Walker," she complained, trying to pull his head between her legs.

Taking pity on her, and wanting to make her forget any trace of the dream she'd had, Trigger let her push his head right where he wanted to go. He licked between her folds, her tangy flavor bursting on his taste buds. That was all it took for him to forget about teasing.

Giving her a few more licks, loving how she squirmed under him, Trigger turned his attention to her clit. Knowing what she liked, and how she got off the fastest, he eased one finger inside her body at the same time he sucked on her clit. Putting his free arm across her belly to hold her down, Trigger ruthlessly worked his woman toward orgasm.

He knew exactly how much pressure to put on her clit, and how hard to finger fuck her. Within a minute, he knew she was on the edge. Usually he'd tease her by easing off then building her up again, but

Trigger's cock was dripping inside his boxers and he wanted to be inside her, to connect with her, more than he wanted to tease.

He knew when she was about to orgasm because every muscle in her body tensed. Her ass lifted off the mattress and she moaned low in her throat. With one last suck on her clit, she hurtled over the edge. Her thigh muscles shook and he could feel her stomach under his arm tighten as she came.

Trigger yanked off his boxers and spread her legs wider to make room for him even as she continued to quake from her orgasm. He notched his weeping cock head to her folds. The heat coming from her felt scalding, but he knew there would be no greater feeling than being buried all the way inside his woman.

Without hesitation, Trigger pushed his way inside her still quivering body, throwing his head back and gritting his teeth to keep from immediately coming at the feel of her inner muscles clenching around his dick.

"Fuck, Di," he panted, holding still inside her, memorizing the feel of her around him.

Looking down, he saw sweat glistening on her forehead, her blonde hair spread across his pillow, and her green eyes looking up at him with love and trust.

"You're always safe with me," he vowed.

"I know," she said, her voice raspy.

"You can't sleep, you stay here in our bed. Turn on a light, read, watch TV, whatever you need to do. But don't leave me so you can suffer alone in the other room."

"Okay," she agreed softly.

Trigger pulled out of her body, grunting at how painful it was to leave her, then thrust back in.

They both moaned.

"More," Gillian begged.

Trigger obliged. He began to fuck her, hard. Her tits bounced on her chest with every thrust and without thought, he reached for them. He pinched her nipples as he made love to her, feeling her clench around him, letting him know she loved what he was doing.

Reluctantly, Trigger let go of her tits, bracing himself above her. The sound of their skin slapping together was loud, erotic. He felt his orgasm approaching way faster than he would've liked.

"Touch yourself," he ordered. "I want to feel you come around my cock."

Gillian didn't hesitate, moving one of her hands between them. His belly hit the back of her hand with every thrust, but she either didn't notice or care.

He could feel her finger flicking against her clit as she did her best to make herself come.

"That's it, Di. God, you're beautiful. I love you so much. You're my everything..."

Trigger was barely conscious of what he was saying; only that he wanted to make sure she knew how much this meant to him. How much *she* meant to him.

"I'm coming!" she cried, but Trigger didn't need the warning. Her inner muscles were practically strangling his dick. It was harder to push inside her now, but he didn't let up.

"Walker!" she exclaimed, and thrusting her pelvis up toward him. Trigger put a hand under her ass and shoved inside her as far as he could get, holding her to him as he finally exploded. It felt as if he would never stop coming.

Trigger didn't want to move. Wanted to stay buried inside the woman he loved more than life, forever. Making sure he didn't crush her, he lowered himself until they were chest to chest. Gillian's legs came up and she hooked her ankles together at the small of his back. They were both breathing hard, and Trigger buried his nose into the space where her shoulder met her neck.

"I love how everything in my house smells like honeysuckle. It's a constant reminder of you. How lucky I am to have you in my life. Please don't shut me out, Gilly." Trigger knew if his teammates could hear him begging, he'd never hear the end of it...but he didn't care. "Knowing you're hurting and you deliberately left our bed, it kills me."

"I won't do it again," Gillian told him.

"Thank you." Trigger lifted his head. "I love you."

"I love you too," she responded.

"Feel better?" he asked.

She gave him a small smile. "Yes."

"I wasn't too rough?" he asked.

"You'd never hurt me."

It wasn't exactly an answer, but with the way she was smiling up at him and clutching him to her, he had to assume the answer was no.

Trigger felt his cock softening and knew it was only a matter of time before he'd slip out of her body. Her hands were clutching his biceps, and he looked over at her left hand. Seeing the diamond ring he'd put there, and knowing soon she'd be his wife, made him sigh in contentment.

Trigger moved to the side then, grimacing when he slid out of her. He pulled Gillian into him, so her head was resting on his shoulder. "What can I do to help you?" he asked.

"You're doing it. Holding me. Making love to me

so amazingly I can't think about anything other than how much I love you."

His arms tightened around her. He'd had no idea how much this woman would come to mean to him all those months ago when he'd first talked to her on the phone. She'd been a terrified victim of a hijacking, but she'd somehow snuck under his radar even then. She hadn't panicked, had done what needed to be done to save herself and a plane load of others as well.

Trigger knew she could do so much better than an overprotective military asshole like him. But he was going to do everything in his power to keep her happy. So she'd never want to leave him.

"Why don't you invite your friends over for a girls' night in tomorrow," he suggested.

"Are you sure?" she asked. "I know it's a pain for you to have to look after us all when we start drinking."

Trigger smiled. Gillian and her three best friends were a handful, but he didn't care. "I'm sure," he told her. "I'd like to think that I can keep your demons at bay all by myself, but I know it would be good for you to have some girl time."

"Agreed. Walker?"

"Yeah, Di?"

"I won't leave our bed again. If I can't sleep, I'll stay here."

"Thank you. Do you think you can sleep now?"

"Yeah. I'm exhausted."

Trigger hugged Gillian closer and knew the exact moment when she fell asleep. Her entire body relaxed against him, and he sighed in relief. It was almost scary how much love he had for the woman in his arms. She was his life. She didn't need him, but he sure as hell needed *her*. He'd spend the rest of his life making sure she knew just how much.

BEST CHRISTMAS EVER

by Susan Stoker

Edited by Kelli Collins
Manufactured in the United States

NOTE FROM THE AUTHOR

Best Christmas Ever is a short story I wrote for a holiday anthology that came out in December 2019 and was only available for a short time.

The two main characters are older, and not looking for love. But sometimes love finds you when you least expect it. (And you might recognize a few characters that you already know and love toward the end as well!)

Enjoy!

-Susan

BLURB FOR BEST CHRISTMAS EVER

WHEN CHRIS and Sienna meet during an accident in Texas, the perfect strangers soon discover they're inexplicably linked...in more ways than one. Coincidence? Perhaps. Or maybe the makings of their very own Christmas miracle.

BEST CHRISTMAS EVER

Part 1, The Accident

SIENNA BERNFIELD DIDN'T EVEN HAVE time to scream. One moment she was driving toward Fort Hood Army post, and the next, the world exploded in front of her midsize rental car.

A huge pickup truck ran a red light and broadsided the Honda civic in front of her. She slammed on the brakes and watched in disbelief as the truck pushed the smaller car across the intersection and pinned it against the side of a brick building nearby.

Acting on instinct, Sienna pulled her car over and leaped out. She raced toward the accident, ignoring the bystanders yelling that the person driving the truck was fleeing the scene. Her only concern was whoever was inside the now crumpled car trapped between the truck's grill and the wall of the building.

As a paramedic back home in Nashville, she knew how important it was to get an injured person help as soon as possible. The "golden hour" was the first sixty minutes after a traumatic injury and was considered the most critical for successful emergency treatment. If the person or persons in the car were hurt, their golden hour had already begun.

The entire passenger side of the car had been smashed in, and Sienna was relieved to find no one sitting there. Christmas music played eerily in the background from a nearby store as she sized up how to get to the driver.

The doors on either side of the car were inaccessible, the passenger side was blocked by the truck, and the driver's side was butted up against the brick building. The windshield was cracked but not busted out, and there was loose glass all over the trunk from the back window.

The morning had been cool, especially for Texas, and Sienna was wearing a long-sleeve blouse and a jacket. Without stopping to think about what she was doing, she climbed up onto the trunk and brushed debris off of the roof, before lying on her belly and peering into the interior of the car through the sunroof.

A man was sitting in the driver's seat, his head leaning against the brick of the building as the window next to him had shattered upon impact. Sienna could see blood trailing down the side of his face and dripping onto his chest. At first glance, she didn't see any bones sticking out of his arms or legs, which was good. But that didn't mean he didn't have internal or spinal injuries.

The steering wheel was bent downward and the man was obviously pinned inside the vehicle. There was no way he'd be able to get his legs loose, not without mechanical assistance from the jaws of life.

Glad once more for her small five-foot-two size, Sienna wiggled her way through the sunroof until she was crouched on the crumbled seat next to the man. She couldn't count the amount of times she'd been the one on the ambulance crew to crawl into storm drains, under vehicles, and into other tiny places. She didn't even thick twice about small spaces anymore.

She reached out and put her fingers on the man's carotid artery—and reflexively jerked her hand back when his eyes popped open.

Immediately, Sienna reached for him and grabbed both sides of his head as best she could in the limited space, trying to keep him still so he wouldn't exacerbate any neck injury he might have. "You're okay, sir. You've been in a car crash, but you're okay," she told him calmly.

He reached up with one hand and gripped her wrist, but didn't try to jerk out of her hold or otherwise move.

Sienna could practically see his brain trying to process what had happened and where he was. She saw the second his situation registered because his breathing sped up and his eyes dilated further.

"I need to get out," he said in a low, controlled voice.

"I'm sorry," Sienna told him, "That's just not possible right now. But you're safe. Cars don't blow up like they do in the movies and television shows. I'm sure the cops and firefighters are on their way. They'll get you out as soon as they can."

"You don't understand," he said in a tone Sienna couldn't read. "I'm claustrophobic. I'm going to lose it if I don't get out of here."

———

Christopher King closed his eyes, trying to block out the fact that he was trapped in the ridiculously small rental car he'd picked up at the Austin airport. He'd reserved an SUV, but when he arrived, he'd been informed that there had been a clerical error and the only thing available for him was this Honda Civic. He made sure the employees knew he wasn't happy, but in the end, there wasn't anything he could do about it, and he'd driven away in the car way too small for his liking.

He was a tall man at six-one, and he couldn't remember the last time he'd even been in a vehicle as small as this one. If it wasn't for the fact his son would be arriving home that afternoon from a nine-month deployment in the Middle East, he would've refused to take the vehicle. But he had to get his ass to the Fort Hood area, check into his hotel, go to the base, and make sure he was at the reception area so he could greet Tony when he arrived with his unit.

It was Christmas Eve, and hearing that his son would be returning tonight had been the best present he could've received. Chris had divorced his ex when Tony was only five years old. He didn't get to watch his son grow up as much as he wanted so he did his best to make the effort to stay involved with his life now, even if that meant traveling hundreds of miles to welcome him home from deployment.

Chris didn't particularly like the holiday season. He wasn't a Grinch, but it wasn't fun decorating his apartment by himself. He didn't have anyone special to buy presents for, other than his son, and no one bought him gifts either.

He worked hard and played hard. He loved to camp in the Smoky Mountains and had recently bought a small hunter's cabin, where he went almost every weekend to relax and wind down from his day job.

He'd worked for the Department of Corrections for most of his life. His current assignment was the Riverbend Maximum Security Institution just outside of Nashville. He hadn't started out wanting to be a prison guard, but over time, he'd found that he enjoyed it...for the most part. But after an incident a few years ago, a riot which had involved most of the prison and where he'd literally come face to face with his own mortality, Chris had made the decision to either change his occupation or figure out a way to retire early.

He was forty-nine. Too young to really retire, and way too old to start over with a new occupation, but since meeting with a therapist hadn't helped his claustrobia, he was at a point where he had to make a decision.

His plan had been to come down to Texas, see his son, then make some changes in his life. Of course, life seemed to always throw him a curveball.

Chris knew he was seconds away from panicking

at the thought of being trapped, but he couldn't stop his reaction. He'd opened his eyes to see a brick wall on one side of him and crumpled metal all around. He couldn't move his legs and just about everything on his body hurt. Nothing felt broken, thank God, but he knew he'd be sore for a long time.

He had no idea where the woman next to him had come from. She hadn't been in the car minutes earlier, but at the moment he didn't much care. He heard her tell him that he was all right, but the only thing he could think about was getting out. *He had to get out.*

"Look at me," the woman ordered.

Chris didn't want to open his eyes because then he'd see the spider-webbed windshield in front of him —which threw him right back to the prison on that fateful day—and the way he was trapped inside the stupid piece-of-shit car he'd been forced to drive.

Her voice gentled as she said, "My name is Sienna. I'm a paramedic. I'm not some crazy woman who decided on a whim to climb into a wrecked car."

Chris heard the humor in her voice and wanted to respond to it, but he was having a hard time getting the violent images of the prison riot out of his head. "I'm Chris," he finally said between pants. "Chris King."

"Do you live around here?"

He knew she was trying to distract him, but it wasn't working. "No. I'm from Tennessee."

"Really? Me too. I live in Nashville. What about you?"

That made him open his eyes in surprise. He couldn't turn his head because she was holding him still, but he moved his eyes in her direction. "Me too." She grinned, and the thoughts of the riot he'd lived through suddenly faded from the forefront of his mind. "You're really from Nashville? You aren't just saying that to try to keep me calm?" he asked.

Sienna smiled. "Nope. I really live there. Have for twenty-five years or so."

"Since you were little?" he asked.

She chuckled, and the low sound echoed around the small space they were occupying. It felt as if she'd wrapped a warm blanket around his shoulders. It was that comforting. He kept his eyes on her face, thankful that she was able to keep his mind occupied.

"Bless you. No. I moved there after I graduated from the University of Tennessee."

"There's no way," Chris said.

"No way, what?" Sienna asked.

"That you're in your forties. Thirty-five, tops."

She laughed again, and once more, where he was and what was happening faded, and all he could see were her beautiful brown eyes. "Thanks. It's my size. Being five-two makes me look younger."

Chris tried to shake his head, but she had too firm a grip on him for him to move even an inch. "No. It's you. You're beautiful."

She blushed, and he had the thought that it was a shame. A woman who looked like Sienna should be used to compliments. Should take them in stride. She had pretty light brown hair with blonde highlights. It was tumbled around her shoulders at the moment and she had a black streak smudged on one cheek. He frowned, wondering if she'd hurt herself climbing into this deathtrap with him.

Just as the thought hit him, he remembered where he was and that he was stuck. He tried to shift in the seat, but his legs were pinned under the steering wheel and dashboard. He felt the pressure of the wheel against his thighs.

Closing his eyes again, Chris felt the terror clawing its way up his throat once again.

"So if you're from Tennessee, what are you doing in Texas? Are you lost?"

Chris desperately wanted her to be able to distract him with her questions. He was still holding on to her wrist and he could feel the steady pulse under his hand. He forced his eyes open once more and found that she'd shifted until she was practically sitting in his lap. The steering wheel was preventing her from actually doing so, but she'd done her best to put her face directly in his line of vision. He vaguely heard people talking from outside the car, but he concentrated on Sienna. She was the only thing keeping him from losing his mind.

"My son is coming home from deployment today."

Her eyebrows shot up. "Really?"

"Really."

"Mine is too. Well, it's my daughter, not my son."

Chris stared at her in disbelief. The thought crossed his mind that everything she was saying was a lie, just to keep him calm, but he doubted she'd lie about something like having a kid. "What are the odds?" he asked.

"Astrominical," she replied dryly. "We've lived in the same city for years. We have kids who are probably around the same age. They're both in the Army. They're probably in the same unit and have been stationed together overseas. Then we were traveling at the same place, at the same time. I'm a paramedic and small and...here we are. It's a Christmas miracle."

When she put it like that, it seemed even more improbable, but he liked the thought of her being his Christmas miracle. She was a gift just for him.

It had been a long time since he'd enjoyed a gift as much as he enjoyed the thought of her being his.

"Guess that means when I get out of here, you have no choice but to let me take you out for lunch or coffee or something," Chris said. His words were teasing and flippant, but he meant them. For some reason, he felt as if they were meant to find each other.

"Deal," she said softly, a sheen of pink flooding her cheeks.

Someone pounded on the top of the car then, breaking the moment.

———

Sienna hated how easily she blushed. She blushed when she was embarrassed. She blushed when someone complimented her, when the guys at the station back in Tennessee teased her. She wanted to come off cool and sophisticated with Chris, but of course she probably looked like a blushing virgin or something instead.

She couldn't believe they both had children in the same unit and they were in Texas for the same reason. It had to be fate...didn't it?

"You guys okay in there?" a voice from above asked.

Sienna looked up and saw a civilian looking down at her from the open sunroof. She nodded. "We're good. What's the ETA on the paramedics?"

"Not sure, but they're on their way. There's a group of Army guys out here. They chased down and caught the other driver. They're keeping him secure until the cops get here."

"Someone needs to relay that the fire department is gonna need extraction tools to get the vic out. There's a probable head or neck injury as well," Sienna told the man, her training kicking in.

Without a word, the man's head disappeared and it was just her and Chris once again. She could hear more people talking outside, but for the moment, it seemed like her and Chris were the only people in the world.

Shifting and ignoring the way her knees and hips were screaming in pain at the awkward position she was in, Sienna looked back at the man in front of her.

In the time it took for her to relay Chris's condition to the other man, he'd sank back into his head. He was shaking and sweaty, and Sienna didn't think it was because of his medical issues. He'd said he was claustrophobic and being pinned in place, with her holding him immobile, couldn't be fun.

"I remember this one time when we rolled up on a scene and realized a kid had crawled into a sewer pipe after a kitten and gotten stuck. Of course, the guys I work with are all big and brawny, there was no discussion about it, I knew I'd be the one who had to go in after him."

Chris hadn't opened his eyes again, but Sienna knew he was listening. Without thought, her thumb began to caress his jawline as she continued. "It was the day after Christmas, and his mom told me he'd been playing with his new handheld game all morning and she'd finally forced him outside for a break. I crawled into that sewer, and I've never been claustrophobic, but I struggled with being inside that tube. I reached the boy and, let me tell you, it was hell trying to back out of there while holding on to his leg. He was kicking and screaming and the sound echoed in that small drain pipe. I thought I would be deaf by the time I got him outside.

"Eventually, I made it to the opening and my team pulled me out by my boots, dragging that little boy with me. We were both covered in mud, and things I don't even want to think about, and instead of thanking me, the boy turned and yelled at me, saying he was playing with the kitty, and I didn't have the right to touch him. His mom hustled him into the house with barely even a thanks, probably to play that damn game he'd gotten from Santa."

Chris's eyes opened at last...and instead of

laughing at her final line, he said, "I was working at my job at the maximum-security prison and there was a riot. I locked myself into the observation room, but the prisoners broke in. They busted out the glass, which looked a hell of a lot like the windshield does right now, until it finally broke. They beat the shit out of me then hauled me to solitary confinement and locked me in. It was dark, and I could hear the yelling and screaming of the riot around me. But the scariest thing was the smell of the smoke from the fires they lit. I knew no one knew where I was, and if the fire got out of control, I'd either be burned alive or would suffocate from the smoke. It felt as if I had been buried alive."

Sienna couldn't let go of his head, but she wanted to hug him more than she wanted anything else in her life. She settled for leaning forward and laying her forehead against his own.

He continued, his voice amazingly steady. "Eventually, the police and SWAT got everything under control and searched the prison cell by cell to secure it, and found me. I'm told I was in there for three hours. It felt like days. I've had issues with small spaces ever since."

Sienna pulled back and looked into Chris's dark blue eyes. He had blond hair that was beginning to turn gray at the temples. He had wrinkle lines around his eyes and mouth, meaning he probably laughed a lot. His nose was crooked, it had obviously been broken in the past, possibly even in the riot he'd talked about. He still held on to her wrist, as if she were a lifeline, and she supposed she was.

"I'm not leaving you until you're out of here," she vowed.

"I'm okay," he said immediately, but Sienna could tell he wasn't.

"Of course you are," she agreed. "Tell me about Tony," she demanded.

He hesitated, then one side of his mouth quirked upward. "You're trying to distract me," he accused.

"Yup," she admitted without prevarication. "So...Tony?"

She watched Chris force himself to change gears and think about his son rather than his predicament. As he talked about how proud he was of Tony and what he did in the Army, she silently assessed him.

His heart rate was a little elevated, but that was normal under the circumstances. His skin had good color and he wasn't cold, which was good. He was talking without issue, so he probably didn't have a collapsed lung. The cut on the side of his head was sluggishly bleeding, but nothing that she was too concerned about. Head wounds typically bled a lot, and if nothing else, the bleeding would help clean it out. He'd need stitches, but those were simple enough to put in. His arms were moving just fine and he had a good grip on her wrist. She couldn't assess his legs from her position and because the steering wheel was in her way, which concerned her somewhat.

"You're not listening to anything I'm saying, are you?" Chris asked after a pause.

Sienna's eyes flew up to his guiltily. "Of course I am."

He chuckled—and she could only stare at him in shock. When he smiled, his entire face lit up. She loved the sound rumbling up from his chest as well.

Ashamed of herself for feeling even the smallest iota of attraction for the man when he was literally trapped by the tons of steel around them, she tried to control herself.

"How old was I when I found out I was going to be a father?" Chris quizzed.

Sienna grinned cockily at him. "Twenty-one. You liked Tony's mom, but weren't sure you wanted to spend the rest of your life with her. But you married her anyway and then your son was born."

"Okay," he agreed disgruntledly. "I guess you were listening."

"I'm a woman," Sienna said smugly. "We can do

more than one thing at a time. How do your legs feel?"

"My feet are tingly," he answered immediately. Then asked, "Is that bad?"

"I won't lie. It's not great, but it's not terrible either. The fact that you can feel them is awesome."

"But I'm stuck."

Not wanting him to get fixated back on that and possibly make his claustrophobia flare again, she said, "I met Randy when I was thirteen and he was seventeen. I didn't know it wasn't appropriate then, and even if I did, I wouldn't've cared. I loved him and thought he loved me too. Turns out, he loved having sex...it didn't matter who he had it with. When I was eighteen, I moved in with him. We thought we were so grown up. When I turned up pregnant, he decided that maybe he didn't want to be an adult after all."

"He dumped you? That asshole," Chris growled. "Miranda and I weren't the best husband and wife, but we always worked together when it came to Tony."

Sienna didn't want to admit how good it made her feel to hear him get pissed off on her behalf. "Yeah, he dumped me. But don't feel sorry for me or my daughter. I moved back in with my parents and they helped me raise Sarah. They encouraged me to go to our local community college. I had plans to be a nurse, but from the first ridealong I did on an ambulance, I was hooked. I loved how the paramedics swooped in to do what they could to keep the person alive until he or she reached the hospital. It was a huge adrenaline rush. I got my EMT license first, then went on to get certified as a paramedic. I haven't looked back since."

"From where I'm sitting, you're good at what you do," Chris said with a small smile.

Sienna returned the grin, but didn't respond verbally. She couldn't believe she was having as powerful feelings as she was toward this man. It was crazy. But she couldn't deny that she wouldn't mind getting to know him better once they went back to Tennessee.

"Thanks," she said after a moment.

They sat there in the cocoon of the wrecked car, staring intently at each other, and Sienna wondered what Chris was thinking.

She opened her mouth to ask, when someone yelled from right outside, startling them both. Tightening her grip on Chris's head, she said, "The cavalry has arrived."

"As far as I'm concerned, it was already here," Chris told her, admiration and something she couldn't read shining in his eyes.

—————

As crazy as it seemed, Chris was almost disappointed that his time with Sienna was interrupted. Twenty minutes ago, he would've done anything to get out of the car, but somehow, Sienna had been able to do something that no therapist had been able to...she'd brought him out of a panic attack simply by touching him and talking to him. She'd redirected his thoughts, which he recognized as a tactic others had tried. In the past, he couldn't stop thinking about being buried alive or suffocating in that damn solitary confinement cell, but even though he was still immobile and still stuck in the damn car, he couldn't think about anything other than her.

She'd begun to sweat and her hair was sticking to her forehead and the sides of her neck. She had to be uncomfortable, hunched over, holding his head and neck still. But her entire attention was focused on *him*, not on her own comfort, or lack thereof.

And he hadn't missed the way her eyes lit up when she'd talked about her daughter. He hadn't missed the way her thumb caressed his neck to try to soothe him. She was professional, as any paramedic would be, but there was definitely something between them. Something more than a public servant helping a citizen in distress.

After the firefighters arrived, things began to happen very quickly. They used their tools to peel back the hood of the car and to separate the body of the vehicle from the engine. Sienna kept him calm and explained what was going on every moment, so he wouldn't get freaked out. The sound of the machines was loud and when they couldn't talk, she kept eye contact with him and constantly brushed her thumb back and forth on his neck, letting him know she was right there.

The second the steering wheel was removed and the pressure was removed from his thighs, he breathed a sigh of relief. His toes were still tingling, but he was no longer trapped.

It wasn't until Sienna's hands around his head were replaced with a C-collar that he panicked.

Refusing to let go of her wrist, he said urgently, "Don't go."

"I'm right here," she soothed. "But I need to get out the way so the paramedics can get you out of here."

The second he had to let go of her wrist, all the other things Chris should be worrying about came crashing back to him. For the several minutes it took for them to carefully lift him out of the car and get him settled on a gurney, he did his best to keep his panic at bay. Once the firefighters began to wheel him toward an ambulance, he couldn't resist the temptation to talk to his rescuer again. He tried to turn his head to look for Sienna, but the collar around his neck prevented it. "Sienna?" he called out.

"I'm right here, don't panic," she said.

He felt her hand on his shoulder as the fire-fighters and paramedics kept moving him toward the ambulance. "Will you find Tony? Tell him what happened? I don't know when I'll be able to get out of the hospital. I might miss him, and I don't want him to think I just didn't show up."

"Of course I will," she said. Sienna's face appeared above his, and he felt her slip her hand into his own. He clutched at her and couldn't believe how right it felt to have her hand in his.

"There's a group of men who stopped to help direct traffic and who called the police. They were also the ones who chased down the jerk who hit you and decided to run. While you were being extracted, I talked to one of them briefly, and he said he'd do what he could to help make sure your son knows where you are and what happened."

Chris glanced over to where Sienna was gesturing, and frowned. A group of six men were standing there. They were all younger than he was and extremely fit.

Irrationally, he didn't like the thought of Sienna

spending time with them...and possibly having them catch her eye before he had the chance.

He looked back up at her. "Go out with me," he blurted.

She blinked in surprise. "What?"

"On a date. When I get out of the hospital, or if that's too soon, when we get back to Tennessee. We both live in Nashville. I want to take you out. Maybe for New Year's." He held his breath, waiting for her answer.

"I was dreading this trip," she told him quietly, staying out of the way of the paramedics. "I love my daughter, but I'm not really all that comfortable on the military base. I don't know all the rules and stuff and I'm paranoid I'm going to make some huge faux pas. I hate doing things like this by myself. It's awkward, and seeing all the other couples waiting for their kids makes me feel like a failure for not being in a relationship myself. But now I understand why I had to come. It was to meet you."

"We need to load him up, ma'am," one of the paramedics said. "We'll be going to Darnall Army Medical Center. It's the closest hospital. He was very lucky that he wasn't hurt more than he was."

Sienna nodded and went to take a step back. Chris tightened his hold on her hand. "Wait!"

The paramedic looked put out, but he didn't insist on getting him loaded right that second.

"You didn't answer my question," Chris told Sienna.

Then she smiled at him, the most beautiful smile he'd ever seen, and said, "Yes. I'd love to go out with you."

"Best Christmas ever," Chris said, and squeezed her hand, wishing he could bring it up to his lips and kiss it. The straps on the gurney kept him imbobile, but for once he wasn't thinking about the fact that he was claustrophobic, he was thinking about where he should take Sienna on their date. The last thing he saw before the doors of the ambulance closed was her beautiful smile.

Part 2, The Angel

"I can't believe you know Tony's dad," Sarah said later that evening as they were on the way to the hospital to see Chris. The Army personnel at the scene of the accident had done just as they'd promised, and had escorted her onto the post. Sienna learned they were in some sort of platoon together, and she got the sense that they didn't want to talk about it, but if she had to guess, she'd say they were Special Forces. They just seemed to have that vibe about them.

She'd also noticed the rings on all their fingers.

She'd seen the jealous look Chris had given them and had wanted to reassure him that she wasn't attracted to the men at all, but she also hadn't wanted to embarrass him. When she saw Chris again, she could tell him the men all seemed to be married... happily so, if their discussions about their wives were any indication.

She'd followed the men's vehicles through the gates and to a building in the middle of the busy Army post. They'd escorted her inside and introduced her to the commander of her daughter's unit. He knew who Tony was, as apparently he was an excellent soldier and had made a positive impression on many of the officers in the unit. He'd had both Tony and her daughter escorted to his office.

Sienna had been overjoyed at seeing her daughter again. FaceTime and emails just weren't the same as seeing your flesh and blood in person. Sienna was happy to see for herself that her daughter was safe and sound. Then she'd welcomed Tony home and told the young man everything that had happened to his dad and what she knew about his medical condition.

Now they were all in Sienna's rental car on the way across the Army post to the medical center.

"It's crazy that you both live in Nashville," Tony said. He was a very polite young man who Sienna had liked from the start. He was about the same age as Sarah, but apparently they didn't really know each other. Even though they'd been deployed together, Tony was infantry and Sarah was a cook, so they didn't run in the same circles while overseas.

"I know, right?" Sienna said. "I thought he was kidding at first. What are the odds that we met down here in Texas, both from Nashville, and with kids in the same unit?"

"It's pretty odd. Maybe it's your Christmas miracle," Tony joked.

"That's exactly what I said!" Sienna laughed.

Then Tony sobered and asked, "You're sure he's okay?"

Sienna nodded and tried to reassure the young man. "I'm sure. He hit his head on the driver's side window, but I think that's the extent of his injuries. He was very lucky."

"I don't understand why he was driving such a small vehicle," Tony mused. "He never rents anything smaller than a full-size car or SUV."

Sienna shrugged. "I don't know, I'm sure he'll tell you when we get to the hospital, but from what I understand, that car saved his life. The side curtain air bags really cushioned him. It could've been a lot worse."

"Thank you for being there for him," Tony told her.

Sienna pulled into a parking spot at the medical center and turned to Tony. "From the little I know of your dad, I have a feeling he would've been just fine even if I wasn't there. He really wasn't hurt all that badly."

"But you said he was trapped," Tony insisted.

Sarah was watching the conversation with interest.

"He was," Sienna confirmed.

"He's claustrophobic. He doesn't like to admit it, but from what he's told me over the last few months while I was deployed, it's getting worse, not better."

"I'm not sure anyone would want to admit something about themselves that could be seen as a weakness," Sienna said. "As a soldier, I'm sure you've seen others who were wounded and who are struggling to deal with the things they've done and seen while deployed. This is no different. Just because your father is having a hard time coming to terms with the riot at the prison doesn't mean he isn't strong or brave. The fact that the first thing he told me was he's claustrophobic makes me respect him more, not less. It's not manly or tough to hide what you're feeling. Remember that."

Tony stared at her for a beat, then his lips twitched. "Yes, ma'am."

Sienna shook her head. "Sorry. As someone who has seen my share of therapists because of what I've seen and done, I tend to be passionate about the subject. Come on, let's go inside and see if we can't find your dad. I know he's probably anxious to see you."

The three headed inside the hospital and were directed to Chris's floor. They went down a long hall and Tony pushed open the door to a room, but Sienna paused before following him inside.

Sarah turned just inside the room and asked, "Mom? Are you coming?"

For a split second, Sienna wondered what she was doing. She and Sarah should be headed to the nearest Chinese restaurant, as was their Christmas Eve custom. She should've dropped Tony off and been on her way.

Why was she excited to see Chris again? It wasn't as if they were actually dating. They were strangers. She'd been first on the scene of an accident more times than she could count.

Why was Chris King so different?

Before she had time to grab Sarah and make an

escape, she heard Chris's happy shout of greeting upon seeing his son. And that was that. Hearing his low, rumbly voice made her feet automatically move forward, as if they had a mind of their own.

Closing the door behind her, Sienna smiled at the scene in front of her. Tony sat on the side of the bed and was embracing his father. Man and son had no problem showing affection for one another. Sienna liked that. The genuine emotion coming from both men was easy to see and feel in the room.

When they were done greeting each other, Chris's eyes met Sienna's. "Hey," he said with a broad smile. "You came back."

"So I did," Sienna said, knowing she was blushing once more, but not able to control it. She felt as if she were fifteen again every time she was around him. She wouldn't have blushed, but the look in his eyes told her that he was just as interested in her as she was in him.

She managed to sit down and have a normal conversation with the others in the room, but Sienna was more than aware of the way Chris kept sneaking looks at her, just as she did at him. The tension between them was so thick, she couldn't believe Sarah and Tony didn't comment on it.

After the tenth time being reassured his dad really was all right and the doctor was only keeping him overnight as a precaution because of a slight concussion, Tony finally stood up. "If you're really all right, dad, I'm going to head out. Some of the single guys from the unit are getting together for an impromptu Christmas/welcome-home party." Tony turned to Sarah. "Wanna come?"

Sarah looked at her mom. "Oh, well...we were going to find a Chinese restaurant and have dinner..."

Sienna shook her head at her daughter. "It's fine. Go on. Have fun. I'll talk to you tomorrow."

"Are you sure?"

Sienna's eyes flicked to Chris, and when she saw that he was staring at her with a look so intense, she immediately flushed. "I'm sure," she said absently, holding eye contact with Chris.

Their connection was severed when Tony leaned over to hug his dad once more. Sienna stood to hug her daughter. Once their children were gone, Sienna immediately felt awkward.

But Chris held out his hand, palm up, and said, "Come here."

———

Chris held his breath as he wanted for the beautiful woman to take hold of his hand. He waited what seemed like hours, but in reality was only seconds. He

81

saw her take a deep breath, then take the few steps needed to bring herself to his side.

The second her fingers closed around his, Chris relaxed. He pulled on her hand until she was standing right next to the mattress. He tugged once more and she sat in the spot that his son had occupied a minute ago. "Thank you for coming with Tony," he told her, wanting to get this part over with before moving on to more interesting topics. "I know he's in his twenties, but he's still my little boy, and I hated that he'd hear about my accident from someone else."

"The commander did a good job in making sure he knew you were fine before I gave him any details," Sienna told him.

Chris loved the sound of her voice. It was low and even, and it made him relax now, just as it had when they were inside the wrecked car earlier. "And thank you for coming up to my room with him."

"You're welcome."

"Are you hungry?" he asked.

"I could eat," she responded.

"Chinese?" he asked with a smile.

She returned the grin. "It's tradition. I'm not the best cook, and one Christmas Eve I worked a twelve-hour shift before I got home and there wasn't much to eat. So I made going out a big game with Sarah. It became a tradition after that. But..."

"But?" he asked when she paused.

"I have a confession," Sienna said seriously.

"Yes?"

"I don't like Chinese food," she whispered. "It was the only restaurant open that Christmas Eve all those years ago."

Chris smiled. Then he laughed. When she giggled in response, he laughed even harder. Before he knew it, they were both guffawing and holding their stomachs from laughing so hard. When they'd both calmed down, he said, "I'd love to be able to cook you a fabulous Christmas Eve dinner, but I'm afraid that's impossible this year."

"Rain check," Sienna said with a shy smile.

Chris felt his heart swell. He had no idea if they'd still be talking in a year, but he sure hoped so. "How about if you order something to go, then we can eat here together. The doctors said I don't have any restrictions on my diet. They really are just keeping me here as a precaution. I'll be discharged in the morning as long as I don't have any pain overnight."

"Sounds good. How do you feel about hamburgers?"

"Whataburger?" Chris asked.

"We're in Texas...what else?" Sienna quipped.

Chris knew he was still holding her hand, but she didn't move to pull it away from him.

After a beat, she asked, "What are we doing?"

"Getting to know each other," Chris said immediately.

"This is crazy," she said more to herself than to him.

"The only crazy thing would be ignoring this intense connection we seem to have," Chris said, taking a risk. "I like you Sienna. A lot. I have no idea what will happen in the future, but for now, I just want to enjoy your company and get to know more about you. What kind of music you like, what your favorite color is, and maybe more about the previous forty-some-odd years that you've lived."

She chuckled, but didn't respond.

"You feel it, right?" Chris asked, suddenly afraid that he was the only one feeling the intense connection between them.

"I feel it. But it's scaring the hell out of me," Sienna admitted.

"I'm a man in a hospital bed with a concussion, what's there to be scared of?" Chris asked with a smile.

At that, she sat up straight and nodded. "You're right."

"Of course I am."

Sienna rolled her eyes. "I'm going to go find a Whataburger and hope it's open. I'll be back."

She stood, but Chris didn't let go of her hand.

He stared up at her, and then nodded. Brushing his thumb across the back of her hand, he finally dropped it. "Hurry back. Drive safe. Watch out for rogue pickup trucks. I hear they can be dangerous."

She smiled at his quip and nodded. Picking up her purse, she headed out of the room and looked back when she was at the door. Licking her lips, she said, quietly, "I'll be back soon."

"Okay."

Chris closed his eyes when she was gone and took a deep breath. He didn't know what it was about Sienna, but he hadn't looked forward to anything in a long time as much as he did her return.

———

Sienna glanced at her watch and was surprised to see it was almost midnight. The night nurse had been in a few times to check on Chris, but was satisfied that he was doing fine. She'd told Sienna that visiting hours ended at ten, but since it was Christmas Eve, she'd look the other way if she happened to stay longer than that.

They'd eaten their hamburgers and had been talking nonstop ever since. Chris was extremely easy to talk to. She felt as if she'd known him for years, rather than less than a day.

"What time is it?" Chris asked.

"Almost midnight."

"Will you grab my backpack for me?"

Sienna blinked at the surprising request. She was sitting on a chair next to his bed, leaning her elbows on the mattress. He'd been lying on his side and they'd formed a sort of intimate bubble over the last few hours.

Doing as he asked, Sienna stood and grabbed his backpack where it sat next to the wall. She handed it to him and watched as he rifled through it. She was curious, but kept quiet. After a moment, he pulled something out, and then leaned over to put the bag on the floor next to the bed. He reached out a hand once more, and automatically, Sienna reached for it.

He encouraged her to sit on the edge of the mattress and gazed up at her with a look so intense, it made Sienna catch her breath.

"Christmas has never been my favorite holiday. Most years I was by myself as Tony was with his mom. The years I did have him, I constantly worried about whether he was comparing the holiday at my house, to the one he usually had with his mom." He shrugged self-consciously. "I put so much pressure on myself to make everything perfect for my son, I never really thought about the meaning of the holiday. That it was a time to be thankful for what you had and to give to others. When Tony graduated from high school, I volunteered to work most holidays, simply because it was less lonely. When I was caught in the middle of that riot, I thought I was done for. That the cops would find my beaten and broken body in that cell and that would be that."

Sienna made a noise of protest in the back of her throat, and Chris reached up and brushed a lock of hair behind her ear.

"You already know that I've been struggling with claustrophobia. I've been kicking around the idea of retiring and finding something else to do. When I was stuck inside that car, the first thought that went through my head, was 'not again.' But then I heard the voice of an angel. *You*, Sienna. You were there. Forcing me to keep it together."

"Chris," she protested, but he put a finger on her lips to shush her. Her lips tingled where his finger touched, and Sienna wanted to open her mouth and take his finger inside, but she tried to concentrate on what he was saying instead.

"Tony gave me this for Christmas when he was ten. He said it was a good luck charm and it would lead me to find my own angel. I've carried it with me every day since." He picked up her hand and placed something in her palm.

Sienna looked down to see a small rock in her hand. A crude angel was painted on the surface, the paint peeling off, but the cute brown-haired angel was recognizable all the same.

"Merry Christmas," he said softly, and wrapped her fingers around the small stone.

The meaning of his words sank in and she gasped, her eyes flicking up to meet his. "I can't take this."

"Yes, you can. Please. I need you to have it. I need to make sure you're safe out there."

The rock seemed to burn a hole in her hand. She'd never been given anything so special before. "I don't know what to say."

"You don't have to say anything," he reassured her. "This feels so right. Like it's meant to be. You're my angel, Sienna. My Christmas angel." After a moment, he wrapped his hand around the back of her neck.

Goose bumps rose on her arms as the calluses on his hand brushed across her sensitive nape.

Chris didn't move, didn't pull her toward him. Didn't pressure her for anything. Simply stared up at her, every emotion easy to read in his eyes and face.

He wanted her. He truly believed she'd been sent to help him out in his time of need. On Christmas Eve at that.

Why *shouldn't* she be his angel? Maybe she *was* sent to be at that exact intersection when he'd needed her. What were the odds that their kids would be in the same Army unit? Or that they lived in the same city?

Throwing caution to the wind, and deciding she was going to go after what she wanted for once in her life, Sienna leaned forward, closing the distance between them. She felt Chris's fingers tighten on the back of her neck and saw his small smile seconds before her lips landed on his.

Sienna had kissed and been kissed many times in her life. Some were good, others not so much. But the Christmas kiss she shared with Chris was more intense, more spine-tingling, more...meaningful than anything she'd ever experienced before.

She closed her eyes and gave herself up to the feelings coursing through her body. She desired him, but she could taste the sweet promise in his lips.

He held her to him firmly, but not so tight that she didn't know he'd let go immediately if she pulled back. Their tongues teased each other for a beat before he slanted his head, taking her deeper. Sienna made a guttural noise at the back her throat and put a hand on his chest to help keep her balance.

How long they made out, she didn't know, but

when he finally pulled back, she whimpered in protest.

When she opened her eyes, she expected to see Chris smiling, or at least looking amused at how pathetic she sounded. But instead when she looked into his gaze, all she saw was tenderness.

"Merry Christmas, Sienna," he said softly.

"Merry Christmas, Chris."

"I still want to take you out for New Year's," he told her.

Sienna could only nod.

Then he licked his lips, and his eyes flicked to her mouth before coming back to meet hers. "I wouldn't change anything about this day. Not one second."

Swallowing hard, Sienna nodded.

"You should go. I'm sure you're tired, and I know you have plans with Sarah tomorrow."

Sienna nodded again.

Chris smiled. "Maybe one more kiss before you go though?"

Liking that he was asking, and not simply taking what he wanted, Sienna leaned forward again.

Twenty minutes later, his number programmed into her phone, and hers in his, Sienna stood in the doorway. Christmas music was softly playing from somewhere down the hall, but otherwise everything was quiet. "I'll talk to you tomorrow," Sienna told

Chris. They'd made out until Chris had pulled away with a groan. She knew she needed to get to her hotel, but the last thing she wanted to do was leave.

"Yes, you will," Chris said.

She could tell he was as reluctant for her to go as she was.

"Text me when you get to your hotel so I know you got there all right?" he asked. "I'll worry if you don't."

"I will." It felt good to be worried about. It had been a long time since someone had cared if she made it home or not.

She fingered Chris's angel stone in her pocket.She didn't know what she'd done in her life to be in the right place at the right time to meet Chris, but she thanked her lucky stars.

Smiling, Sienna backed the rest of the way out of the hospital room and turned to walk down the hallway, a huge smile on her face.

She had no idea what their future held, but she had a good feeling about it. About him. About *them*.

That night, she had a dream. She and Chris were sitting in a pair of rocking chairs, holding hands, watching the sun set over the ocean. Sarah and Tony were there with what she assumed were their spouses, and there were kids running around everywhere. Chris turned to her, and the look of love in his eyes was as clear and familiar to her as anything she'd ever seen.

"I love you, Mrs. King."

"And I love you, Mr. King," she returned.

Sienna woke up smiling and reached for the angel rock Chris had given her the night before. She clutched it in a fist and held it to her chest. "Thank you for sending him to me," she whispered. "Merry Christmas."

———

May you have the "Best Christmas Ever" this year and every year!

-Susan

FIRST KISS

by Susan Stoker

NOTE FROM THE AUTHOR

First Kiss is a brand new story that I wrote about Annie and Frankie's first kiss. It's been fun to "watch" Annie grow up and see her relationship with Frankie stay strong.

If you haven't "met" Annie or Frankie before now, these are the books that you might want to pick up.

Marrying Emily (Where you meet Annie)
Protecting Kiera (Where you meet Frankie)
The Gift (Where Annie & Frankie meet for the 1st time)
First Kiss (Annie & Frankie's first kiss)
Rescuing Annie (The "rest of the story" This book hasn't been published yet, but it's in the works!)

Annie also pops up in quite a few of the Delta Force

Heroes series (the books that start with "Rescuing" and you see glimpses of her in the Delta Team Two series (the books that start with "Shielding").

I love Annie and Frankie as a couple. They were "made" for each other.

I hope you enjoy their story...and are looking forward to Rescuing Annie to come in the future.

~Susan

BLURB FOR FIRST KISS

Annie Fletcher is far more tomboy than girly-girl; Frankie Sanders has a disability most boys don't have to endure. But in each other's eyes, they're perfect—and the teen sweethearts have waited nearly a decade for their first kiss.

If they can find more than a few minutes alone during his holiday visit, Frankie and Annie's Christmas promises to be the most magical ever.

CHAPTER 1

"DAD!" Annie yelled the second the front door of her house slammed behind her. "Are you ready yet?" This had been the longest day ever, and not only because it was the last day of school before holiday break.

Frankie was coming to visit today.

Annie knew her friends thought she was crazy for being so serious about a boy who lived all the way on the other side of the country, in California. That she'd never once been tempted to date anyone else. That she claimed to love him, even though they'd never spent more than a week or so together at a time.

Annie *did* love Frankie. Period. She'd decided when she was seven or eight that she was going to marry him, and nothing in the almost decade since had changed her mind. She talked to him on the phone as much as her parents would let her, and they emailed and messaged all the time.

Her parents had talked to his dad, and they'd all agreed that he could come out to visit her for a week before Christmas. His plane was supposed to land in an hour and a half, and it would take almost that amount of time to get down to the airport in Austin. The last thing Annie wanted was to be late.

Her stomach was doing flip-flops in anticipation of seeing him again. They FaceTimed regularly, but it wasn't the same thing as seeing Frankie in person.

"Dad!" she yelled again, dropping her backpack on the floor. Normally she was careful to hang it up or bring it to her room, but at the moment, all she wanted was to get in the car and start heading south.

"There's no need to yell," her mom said calmly as Annie entered the large living room attached to the kitchen. Emily Fletcher was standing by the sink rinsing dishes and putting them into the dishwasher.

"Mom!" Annie said in exasperation. "We're gonna be late! Please tell me Dad's home from work," she pleaded.

"He's home."

Annie sighed in relief.

But then her mom continued, "He got home about five minutes ago. He's in the shower and will be down in ten minutes or so."

Annie groaned.

Emily's lips twitched. "So dramatic," she told her daughter. "Rayne and Harley already came over and picked up your brothers, so we don't have to wait for them."

Annie rolled her eyes and headed for the stairs, but she was very thankful her little brothers weren't around to slow them down. John was two, Doug was six, and Ethan was ten. Ethan and Doug were super excited to see Frankie as well, though John was too young to really know him yet. And while she loved her brothers, she was relieved her mom's friends had already picked them up.

Since her dad wasn't ready to go yet, she'd take the time to change and freshen up. Normally, she didn't care too much about her clothes and hair, but she wanted to look her best for Frankie.

Ripping off her shirt as soon as her door closed behind her, Annie stood in front of her closet for a long minute, trying to decide what to wear. She sighed. She didn't like fancy frou-frou clothes. Never had. Most of her stuff was black, army green, or khaki. There were no frills or lace on anything. Then, glancing down at her chest, Annie pressed her lips together. Most of the time she didn't mind that she didn't have big boobs. They would've made the obstacle course more difficult. But she desperately wanted Frankie to be attracted to her, and from what she could tell from the boys at school, they liked boobs. Big ones.

Shaking her head and refusing to go down the self-deprecation rabbit hole, Annie reached out and grabbed a black short-sleeve shirt. It wasn't a T-shirt, which was what she normally lived in, but it hopefully wouldn't give off vibes that she was trying too hard to impress Frankie.

She pulled the shirt over her head, and made a split-second decision. She took off her jeans and reached for a black miniskirt her mom had gotten for her a year or so ago that she'd never worn. Annie wasn't a skirt kind of person at all, but today was a special occasion.

Lately, her and Frankie's late-night talks had become more intimate. Nothing over the top, but he'd told her how pretty he thought she was, and how he couldn't wait to hold her. Annie, in turn had admitted that she'd had dreams about kissing him.

Her friends made fun of her because she'd never even kissed a boy. But the only person she wanted to get that intimate with was Frankie. And since he wasn't here, she refused to give in to peer pressure and kiss any ol' boy who came along.

Annie pulled on the combat boots she wore with practically everything and studied herself in the mirror. Her long dirty-blonde hair was pulled back in a messy knot at the base of her head, her blue eyes seemed to sparkle with excitement, and she'd been working on building up her arm muscles by doing pullups and pushups, giving her some impressive biceps as a result. Though her dad and the rest of his team went out of their way to remind her often that she was beautiful exactly the way she was, giving her confidence in her looks.

Cocking her head, Annie decided that maybe the black shirt, skirt, *and* boots was a bit much.

She turned to her closet and spied a red shirt in the back. Reaching for it, she held it up and contemplated if she had the guts to wear it or not. It was a scoop neck with cap sleeves. There was a tie at the end of each sleeve, giving it a more feminine look.

Taking a deep breath, Annie brought it over to her bed and laid it down. She took off the black top she'd just put on and exchanged it for the red one.

This time, when she went to look in the mirror, she smiled. The red on black was still bold, still her style, but the femininity of the blouse made her feel...pretty.

She reached up and pulled out the scrunchie in her hair and quickly ran a brush through the long strands. Mentally nodding, she turned away from the mirror and headed out into the hall. She went to her parents' bedroom door and knocked.

"Dad? You almost ready?"

"Just about, sprite," her dad called through the door.

"Do *not* call me that when Frankie is here," Annie ordered through the door. The nickname made her feel special, but she didn't want Frankie hearing it and thinking of her as a little kid.

The door opened and Annie looked up at her dad. Fletch had adopted her when he'd married her mom, and he was the best thing to happen to both of them. She loved this man more than she could ever say.

"You look beautiful," her dad said with a scowl on his face.

Annie couldn't help but laugh. "Don't look so happy about it," she teased.

Fletch chuckled and reached out and pulled Annie into his embrace.

She allowed it, as she loved the feel of her dad's arms around her. He always made her feel safe.

"I'm not sure I'm ready for you to be so grown up," he murmured into her hair.

"Dad," she complained. "I'm sixteen. Not eight anymore."

"I know." He pulled back and put his hands on her shoulders. "You might be sixteen, but that doesn't mean you're an adult. And while I like Frankie, and agreed that he could come visit. I have to remind you that at no time are you allowed to be behind a closed door with him."

Annie rolled her eyes. "I know, Dad. You already told me that."

"I just want to make sure you remember. I was his age once, and trust me, he's gonna take one look at you and his hormones are gonna go out of control."

Annie giggled. She shook her head. "Frankie's not like that. He's respectful of me and my boundaries. He'd never pressure me to have sex, especially not when he's staying in your house."

"He'd better not," her dad muttered.

Annie wasn't worried in the least. Heck, sex wasn't even on her radar right now. "Stop worrying, Daddy," she said, doing her best to put her dad at ease. "It'll be fine. Are you ready? Can we go now?"

Fletch leaned in and kissed her forehead before nodding. "I'm ready. Your mom just finished getting the pot roast in the Crock-Pot before you got home."

"It smells awesome," Annie said. "And she was finishing up the dishes earlier, so she should be ready." Looking at her wrist and seeing how much time had gone by since she'd gotten off the bus, her eyes widened. "Shoot, look at the time! We need to go, Dad! Frankie's gonna think we forgot him!"

"He's not going to think that," Fletch said, unperturbed by his daughter's angst. "How many times have you messaged him today?"

"A few," Annie mumbled, thinking about the twenty texts she'd sent in the last couple of hours. She knew he couldn't read them when he was in the air, but she couldn't help but let him know how excited she was for him to get there.

"All right, sprite...er...Annie. Sorry, I'm trying," he said when she glared at him. "Let's go get your mom and we'll be on our way."

Annie turned and headed down the hall toward the stairs, but her dad's words stopped her.

"Frankie's a lucky guy," he said softly.

Annie shook her head as she looked back at her dad. "*I'm* the lucky one, Dad. Not many girls find the boy they're gonna marry when they're seven."

Then she turned and raced down the stairs, yelling at her mom that Dad was finally ready and to get a move on.

CHAPTER 2

FRANKIE WAITED IMPATIENTLY in the back of the plane as everyone in front of him took their damn sweet time getting their bags and shuffling forward. His phone had vibrated like crazy once he'd turned it back on when they'd landed, and he couldn't help but smile at seeing all the texts from Annie.

She'd texted when she was in her last class, when she was on the bus, when she got home, when she left home to head to the airport, when they arrived—including one about how her dad was driving her crazy, trying to find the closest parking spot he could—then finally, how she was standing at the bottom of the escalator in the baggage area waiting for him.

She'd taken a closeup selfie of herself with the escalator behind her, smiling huge, with the caption, *I can't wait to hug you!*

Frankie had a hard time believing this beautiful, outgoing, popular, and amazing girl liked *him*. When he looked in the mirror in the morning, he had to wonder what on earth she saw when she looked at him. His dad kept telling him that he'd grow into his body, but right now he was gangly as hell. He was doing his best to work out, to put some muscle mass on his chest and arms, but so far he hadn't seen much improvement.

Not to mention the fact that he was disabled. His dad didn't like that word, and told him over and over that he was as capable as anyone else. His lack of hearing didn't define him and wouldn't be a hindrance unless he allowed it to be.

In the sixth grade, he'd gotten a cochlear implant, which allowed him to more easily function in the hearing world, but the device on his head just above his ear made it obvious that he was different from others. Not to mention the way he sounded. Frankie had worked very hard in the last few years to speak normally, but he'd always sound different from people who'd been able to hear their entire life.

But not once had Annie made him feel as if his lack of hearing made him weird or different. From the first time they'd met, she'd treated him as if the fact he couldn't hear was special. Unique. She'd started learning sign language that very day. He'd fallen head over heels for her there and then.

He hated that they lived so far away, but that hadn't kept their relationship from blossoming and growing as they got older. This trip was his Christmas present from his dad. He was going to get to spend a whole week with Annie and her family. Frankie couldn't keep the huge smile from his face.

Finally, it was his turn to deplane, and he sent a quick text to Annie, letting her know he was on his way.

Butterflies swirled in Frankie's belly as he headed down the crowded hallway of the airport toward the baggage area. Would they still have the same crazy chemistry they'd had the last time they'd seen each other in person? Will she change her mind about wanting to date him? A long-distance relationship wasn't easy, and Frankie had vowed a long time ago to always make Annie feel special and loved, even if he couldn't be there with her.

He knew she had plans to go to college, be a part of ROTC there, and eventually join the Army. He was more than all right with following wherever her career led her. He'd move to the moon if that was what she wanted to do. Frankie would do whatever it took to make sure she knew he supported her uncon-ditionally.

Taking a deep breath as he stepped onto the escalator, Frankie kept his eyes glued downward, searching for Annie.

At first, his eyes went straight past her. His Annie wouldn't be wearing a skirt. But immediately, he whipped his gaze back to the absolutely radiant girl wearing red and black. God, she looked so amazing.

Annie waved and ran toward the escalator. Laughing, she tried to run up the stairs to meet him, but she wasn't making much progress. Frankie hurried down the steps toward her—and then she was in his arms.

She smelled so damn good. That was one thing he missed with their long-distance chats. Strawberries and peaches would always remind him of Annie. He'd told her that once, and she'd merely laughed and said it was only her lotion.

Feeling her strong body against his own made Frankie long to do more than simply hug her. Lately, he'd been having more intimate thoughts about his Annie, and he worried that he'd do or say something to embarrass her. Pulling back, he smiled down at her. Her long hair seemed to have a mind of its own, clinging around his arms as if it didn't want to let him go.

"Hi," he said.

"Hi," Annie returned a bit shyly.

Frankie wondered about that, as she'd never been shy with him before.

"Good to see you." Fletch's deep voice sounded from behind his daughter.

Frankie reluctantly let go of Annie and turned to her dad. "You too," he told him.

"You look good," Emily said as she leaned in for a hug.

Frankie loved Annie's family. Her mom and dad were awesome, and her little brothers were energetic, happy kids. They'd all welcomed him with open arms...although he had a feeling her dad wouldn't be thrilled if he knew how much Frankie thought about his little girl in a not-so-innocent way. It wasn't that Frankie wanted to have sex with Annie right that second—he wanted their first time to be special—but he definitely wanted to make sure she knew that he wanted more than friendship.

The gift he'd bought for her with his own money seemed to be burning a hole in his pocket. He hadn't dared put it in his checked luggage, and even the idea of putting it in his carry-on had stressed him out. Someone could steal his backpack. No, it was safe and sound in his pocket.

"Flight okay?" Fletch asked.

Frankie nodded. He felt Annie's hand slip into his own, and he smiled at her. God, this girl was perfect.

She obviously wasn't embarrassed to hold his hand in front of her parents, which made him feel all warm and fuzzy.

"Well, let's go find your bag and we'll head home. I made a pot roast for dinner. I hope that's all right," Emily said.

Frankie nodded immediately. "I can't wait." And he couldn't. His dad tried, but he wasn't the best cook in the world. He knew he'd be fed extremely well while he was in Texas for the next week.

Fletch and Emily walked behind him and Annie as they headed into the baggage area. Annie talked nonstop, as if she had to get out everything she'd done since the last time they'd seen each other in the next five minutes.

Frankie merely smiled and nodded as she babbled. She supplemented her words with modified sign language with her free hand. She could've dropped his hand to use ASL properly, but he wasn't upset in the least that she didn't seem to want to let him go.

His Annie was adorable...and she might not see the glances other teenage boys shot her way as they walked through the crowd, but he did.

Frankie stood taller when he was with his Annie. *She* did that for him. People didn't seem to stare at him as much when she was with him, maybe because their gazes were drawn to her instead. He was all right with that. He was happy to let her have the limelight. He'd stand behind her and be her support. His Annie was born to do great things, and he felt lucky to be the man at her side.

————

Dinner that night was crazy, chaotic, and Frankie had never been happier. He loved watching the Fletchers interact. At home, it was just him and his dad, and things were always quiet and calm. Not here. John, being only two, was quite the handful, and the other two boys were constantly trying to outtalk each other.

Emily and Fletch did their best to keep some sort of control, but they definitely had their hands full with their exuberant boys. Annie sat next to Frankie at dinner, and they both kept meeting each other's gazes.

Frankie had never been more relieved to see the interest in his girl's eyes. She'd scooted her chair closer to his, so their thighs were almost touching. And while they both kept their hands to themselves, it was more than obvious to Frankie that Annie was feeling the same crazy attraction he was.

At one point during dinner, Annie reached over and took his hand in hers once more. She'd changed into a pair of jeans when they'd gotten home, so they could play in the backyard with her brothers, but he'd still felt the heat of her skin against the back of his hand when she'd rested their clasped hands against her leg.

After dinner, and after he'd read John and Doug a story, he and Annie went out onto the back deck to relax and talk while her parents stayed inside and watched TV. The lights from the Christmas tree winked and twinkled through the window as they enjoyed the balmy December Texas weather.

"I can't believe you're here," Annie told him. They were sitting side by side in the loveseat swing on the deck and were once more holding hands.

"Me either. But it feels as if I was just here. Except for the fact that Doug is a year older than when I last saw him. And I swear Ethan has grown a foot since then too."

"Yeah, they're growing like weeds. Mom complains about how much they eat, but I know she really doesn't care," Annie said.

"I didn't really get to say it earlier, but you looked amazing when I saw you at the airport," Frankie told her.

He could see her blush even in the dim light coming from inside. "It was the skirt."

Frankie shook his head. "No, it wasn't. As much

as I loved seeing you in it, it was you. You could've been wearing a ratty old T-shirt and sweats and I would've thought you were just as beautiful."

Annie licked her lips, and Frankie couldn't help but stare at them. He was very cognizant of her parents sitting just inside, though. And the last thing he wanted to do was something that would make them distrust him around their daughter. He'd never disrespect her or her parents that way.

But that didn't mean he didn't long to taste her lips. To kiss her the way he'd dreamed of more and more recently.

"So...did you go to the Christmas dance with that girl?" Annie asked.

Frankie blinked in surprise. "You mean Jenny?"

"Yeah. Her."

"No, of course not. I went with some of my friends, but we left early because it was boring. I have no desire to date anyone else, Annie. Do you?"

"No," she said without hesitation, making him feel a lot better.

"So we're exclusive. Boyfriend, girlfriend?" he asked, needing the confirmation. Frankie wasn't dumb. His Annie could have any guy she wanted. They'd probably line up outside her door to date her if she was open to it.

"Yes."

"Good."

"Frankie?"

"Yeah?"

"I'm glad you're here. I missed you."

Her words felt good. *Damn* good. "I missed you too."

"The week's gonna go too fast."

It would, Frankie had no doubt about that.

Annie leaned into his side and he put his arm around her shoulders. They sat that way for a long time, neither speaking, just enjoying being in the same physical space.

Eventually, Emily poked her head out of the door and said, "It's getting late."

Frankie wouldn't have minded sitting outside with Annie all night, but her mom's words were a clear statement that it was time to come inside.

Forty minutes later, Frankie lay in the bed in the Fletchers' guest room and stared at the ceiling. The present he'd bought for Annie sat on the small table next to the bed. He didn't know when he'd give it to her, but he wanted to wait for exactly the right moment.

CHAPTER 3

"HAVE FUN YOU GUYS," Emily said, as Annie climbed out of the car with Frankie at her heels. "I'll be back at four to pick you up. Please be ready."

"We will, Mom," Emily told her. They were at the mall, and they had three hours to hang out together so Annie could finish up her Christmas shopping. Her brothers were busy elsewhere that afternoon— Doug was hanging out at a trampoline park with his friends and Ethan was at a birthday party. Her dad was on post, at work with his team, and her mom was going to bake cookies while John napped.

The Fletchers' schedule was always crazy busy, especially around the holidays when everyone was home from school. Annie was grateful for a few hours to be with Frankie without her family around. She loved them, but they were exhausting sometimes.

They walked slowly around the mall, and Frankie didn't complain even once when she wanted to go into every knickknack store. Annie didn't care much for clothes shopping, but she loved to browse the toy store, the greeting card store...even the funky store at the very end of the building that sold tie-dye shawls and smelled a little funky from whatever incense they were burning.

Annie found a few things for her brothers and her parents, and even found the most perfect gift for Truck, one of her dad's teammates. But the best thing about the afternoon was spending it with Frankie. Laughing and talking, and knowing they still had a few more days to spend together. Refusing to think about how he would be leaving to go home to California way before she was ready to say goodbye, Annie concentrated on the here and now.

As they shopped, he held her hand, carried her bags for her even though she was more than capable of carrying them herself, and made her laugh. Frankie never made her feel awkward, never made her feel as if she was too tomboyish or not girly enough. And she very much liked the admiration she saw in his eyes when he thought she wasn't looking.

They hadn't seen anyone she knew from school until they went into the food court. They got in line to get an ice cream when Annie saw Silas and Mikey approaching. They were two boys in her class who had been a pain in her ass for years. She still remembered when they were at an organizational day on the army post a few years ago, and they'd told her in no uncertain terms that girls should stick to things like cooking and crafts, that they were slower and weaker than boys.

She'd met Aspen Mesmer that day, who was now married to a Delta Force operative, but at the time, she was a medic attached to a Ranger unit. Annie had been enamored of her, and she'd decided right then and there that she wanted to be a medic too.

But ever since then, Mikey and Silas had delighted on picking on her. They were nothing but bullies—and they were the last two people she wanted to see today when she was so deliriously happy with Frankie.

"What's wrong?" Frankie asked.

Annie smiled a little; he always seemed to be able to read her so well. "Nothing. It's just two boys from school that I can't stand."

Frankie opened his mouth to respond, but Mikey had spotted them and strolled up to where they were standing in line with a smirk on his face.

"If it isn't little Annie Oakley. And with a boy. Shit, we all thought you were a lesbian."

Every time Mikey or Silas had given her shit for

not going to parties or the school dances, she'd told them that she had a boyfriend who lived in California, and she didn't want to hang out with any other boys.

Annie rolled her eyes. Seriously, they were all too old for this kind of crap. "There's nothing wrong with being a lesbian, but I've told you over and over that I have a boyfriend, so you shouldn't be surprised. This is him."

Annie knew she'd erred as soon as she finished speaking. She'd put the spotlight right on Frankie, when she should've deflected. But it was too late now.

"Riiiight," Silas sneered as he turned to Frankie. "The nonexistent boyfriend. How much she pay you to come to the mall with her today and pretend to be dating her?"

"I'm Frankie, and I *am* her boyfriend," Frankie said calmly.

Annie thought Mikey's eyes were going to bug out of his head when he heard Frankie speak. He'd come a long way since getting his cochlear implant, but his speech pattern would always be different from that of hearing people.

"Oh my God, he's a retard!" Mikey exclaimed, then burst out laughing.

Annie dropped Frankie's hand and actually took a step toward the laughing duo, but Frankie grabbed her around the waist and pulled her back into his side before she could deck one or both of the idiots.

"Fuck you," she hissed. She'd never been one to swear much—neither of her parents liked when she did—but this was one case when she didn't even try to hold back. "You're both idiots. That word is so repulsive and offensive, but you don't care, do you? Of course you don't. Frankie is *deaf*, not mentally disabled."

"And look, he's got some sort of antenna on his head. You talking to aliens or something?" Silas asked, ignoring her explanation.

"Yup. And I just gave them your names as the first two people to pick up and do anal probes on," Frankie said without missing a beat.

Silas looked surprised for a second at Frankie's comeback, then rolled his eyes. "I'm not surprised Annie can't do any better than a freak like you."

That was it. Annie dropped the bag she was holding and turned to Frankie and quickly signed. *Please let me take him out. I can do it, no problem.*

No, Frankie signed back, not even needing to let go of the bags he was holding to speak. *He's just baiting you. Besides, I don't give a shit what an asshole like him thinks about me, or us.*

"Are you guys having a spasm? Should we call 9-1-1?" Mikey taunted.

Annie turned to him, and slowly and clearly signed, *You're an asshole. I hope you fall into a pit of fire ants and die a slow, torturous death.*

It felt good to tell him exactly how much she hated him, even if he couldn't understand her. Frankie chuckled from next to her, and Annie looked up at him and smiled.

"What'd you just say to me?" Mikey demanded.

"Oh, but I was just having a *spasm*," Annie told him in a patronizing tone.

The lady standing in front of them in line chuckled, making Annie smile even wider.

But that obviously pissed off Mikey. He hated not having the upper hand, and even though he was a jerk and not all that bright, he definitely understood that the woman was laughing at him.

He took a step toward Annie—and Frankie immediately morphed from the laid-back, easygoing guy he'd been seconds earlier into a pissed-off, protective boyfriend.

He dropped the bags he was holding and pushed Annie behind him a step. He held up a hand palm out, as if to block Mikey, and said, "I don't think you want to take us on. First of all, Annie could kick your ass with one hand tied behind her back, and I think you know it. Maybe you and your friend could overpower her if you worked together, but it would be all over your school that the only way you could beat a girl was if you ganged up in an unfair fight.

"But more than that—you know who her dad is. And who his friends are. Trust me, you don't want to be on the wrong side of Cormac Fletcher and his buddies. Not to mention the fact that wanting to hit a girl makes you repulsive, and says a lot more about *you* than it does her. Step. Back. Asshole."

Annie stared at Frankie in disbelief. She knew she shouldn't take her eyes off Mikey and Silas, but she couldn't help but see Frankie in a new light. She'd never seen this side of him...and had to admit that she liked it. A lot. He was right, she could totally take Mikey. Probably both him *and* Silas. Her dad had taught her self-defense, and she'd spent years learning from him and his friends how to fight, even when the people she was up against didn't fight fair.

But having Frankie stand up for her made her love him all the more.

"Whatever," Silas mumbled. "Come on, Mikey. We'll leave the bitch and her retarded boyfriend alone."

Annie's teeth clenched. She *hated* that word.

Mikey narrowed his eyes in her direction and said, "Watch your back, Annie. You've got an ass-beating coming—and I'm gonna be the one to put you in your place."

Annie wasn't scared of Mikey. "Bring it," she told him defiantly.

When the two boys had stalked off, Annie sighed. "I'm sorry," she told Frankie.

"You have nothing to be sorry about. But you *do* need to be careful."

"I will. It seems that just because I'm tough and can take care of myself, it makes me more of a target for guys like them, who think all women should be meek and mild."

"I, for one, love that you're tough."

Annie smiled up at him. "Thanks."

Frankie leaned over and picked up their bags. "Come on, the line's moving. I need to get my girl some ice cream."

"With sprinkles?" Annie asked, putting the two bullies out of her mind. They weren't worth the brain space to worry about.

"Of course," Frankie said. Then he blew her mind by leaning over and kissing her temple, as she'd seen her dad do to her mom a million times. "Only the best for my girl."

Frankie might not be the kind of boy many girls would be attracted to. He was tall and skinny, with the cochlear implant device on the side of his head and his unusual speech pattern. So at first glance, he didn't seem like much of a catch. But Annie was sure he would grow into his body. And she didn't care one whit about his being deaf. She knew the heart of this man was pure gold, and if she lived to be four hundred and thirty-one, she'd never meet another person who she loved as much as she did him.

Twenty minutes later, they were sitting at a table in the food court. They'd finished their ice cream and were killing time before Annie's mom came to pick them up in fifteen minutes or so. Besides Mikey and Silas being jerks, the afternoon had been perfect.

They were talking about nothing in particular when a strange noise caught her attention behind her.

Annie turned to see Mikey had stood up so fast, his chair had crashed to the ground. She immediately rolled her eyes and turned back around, determined to ignore whatever stunt Mikey was pulling to try to get attention now.

But Frankie's gaze was glued over her shoulder.

"Ignore them," she pleaded. "They're just trying to be in the limelight, as usual."

Frankie didn't answer her, instead abruptly standing and heading for Mikey and Silas.

Shocked, Annie turned to stare after him, wondering what in the world he was doing. He'd been the one to encourage her to brush off their words, and he hadn't seemed all that affected by their crude words earlier. Had he changed his mind, wanting to get into a fight with them now?

Confused about what was happening, Annie stood, ready to defend Frankie and fight at his side if need be.

But Frankie wasn't heading toward them for a fight. Far from it.

Mikey was standing by a table with his hands clutched around his throat. His eyes were huge, and even Annie could see the panic on his face.

"He's choking! Someone do something!" Silas exclaimed.

Frankie was there in seconds. He physically turned Mikey so his back was to his front, then he wrapped his arms around the other boy. He quickly and efficiently performed the Heimlich maneuver. After several thrusts, a piece of food flew out of Mikey's mouth, landing with a disgusting splat on the tile floor.

Frankie kept his arms around the boy for a heartbeat, making sure he wasn't going to fall to the ground and hurt himself, before slowly letting go. He kept one hand on his shoulder and moved around him so he could see Mikey's face. "You okay?" he asked.

Mikey nodded as he took in great big gulps of air.

His lips had begun to turn blue, but as Annie watched, color slowly seeped back into them.

"Sit," Frankie insisted, pulling out another chair at the table where Mikey had been sitting earlier.

Mikey did so without hesitation. Then he looked up at Frankie and said, "You saved my life. I couldn't breathe."

Frankie simply nodded.

"Should I call for an ambulance?" a man nearby asked.

Mikey shook his head. "No, I'm good now."

"You sure?" the man asked. "You were turning blue."

"I'm sure," Mikey said.

"Okay."

And just like that, things around them went back to normal. Conversations started back up and people began eating again, as if they hadn't been interrupted by someone almost dying right in front of their eyes.

Frankie squeezed Mikey's shoulder then turned to head back toward Annie.

"Hey!" Mikey called out.

Frankie hesitated, then turned his head to look at the other boy.

"Thanks. I'm sorry about the retard thing."

Annie held her breath. As far as she knew, Mikey had never apologized for anything he'd said or done in his life. He was a bully through and through. But obviously almost dying had scared the shit out of him. Enough to be a good person long enough to actually thank Frankie for saving his life.

"You're welcome," Frankie said, then turned his back on the boys and returned to where Annie was standing by her chair.

"You ready to go wait outside for your mom?" Frankie asked, as if he hadn't literally just saved a life.

Annie nodded. She felt kind of off-kilter. She was the one who wanted to be a combat medic. And she'd turned her back on someone who needed medical attention. She'd let her personal feelings get in the way of paying attention to her surroundings. Of doing what was right.

But Frankie hadn't. Even though Mikey had made fun of him and had even threatened her, he hadn't hesitated to go to his aid.

It wasn't until they were standing outside that Annie had collected her thoughts enough to speak. As soon as Frankie put down the bags he was holding, she snuggled into him, holding on tight as she said, "I'm so proud of you. You acted without prejudice. I probably would've let my feelings about him get in the way, and he could've died."

Frankie immediately shook his head. "I don't believe that for a second. I was facing him and figured out what was happening before you had a chance to. You wouldn't have let him die, Annie. I know that."

Looking up at him, Annie licked her lips. She loved this guy so much. Only *he* could make her nemesis actually apologize for the nasty things he'd said. She was sure Mikey would go back to his normal asshole self tomorrow. But for today, he'd actually shown some decency.

Annie saw Frankie's eyes go to her lips...and she went up on her tiptoes, wanting his kiss more than she wanted anything in the world. But before they could connect, a loud car horn sounded from behind them. Turning her head, Annie saw her mom pulling up to the curb.

"Her timing sucks," Annie complained as she pulled away from Frankie a fraction.

But for a second, his arms didn't let go of her, holding her against him. "I'm not leaving Texas until I get to kiss you," Frankie said.

Annie beamed. "Good," she told him. "But maybe we can wait until my mom's not watching."

Frankie nodded and reluctantly lowered his arms from around her, bending over to grab the bags. Then he reached out a hand and Annie took it in hers, happier than she could remember being for a very long time.

CHAPTER 4

THREE DAYS LATER, Frankie was extremely frustrated. He loved the Fletcher family. They were chaotic and fun and there was always something going on in their house. Annie's three brothers had more energy than he ever remembered having at their age. They constantly roped their sister, and him, into playing with them. Sometimes it was board games, other times it was hide and seek in the yard, and when they did sit down for a moment, it was with a book in their hands, asking someone to read to them.

As a result, other than a stolen moment here and there, Frankie hadn't found the time to give Annie the present he'd brought for her. Nor had he managed the courage to kiss her either. And man, did he want that kiss. He hadn't thought about anything else since they'd been outside the mall, and she'd shown him she wanted his lips on hers by going up on her tiptoes against him.

He was leaving tomorrow to go back to California, and tonight was his last chance to both kiss her and give her the present. He dreaded leaving, but not because he thought it would change the nature of their relationship. He'd miss her. Bad. Annie was it for him. Period. And he was fairly certain she felt the same way.

The weather in this part of Texas was normally fairly mild, even in December, but tonight, a cold front had moved through and the wind was blowing quite hard. It was too chilly to sit outside on the deck like they'd done throughout the last week. Frankie was stressed because that was nearly the only time they'd been alone.

But amazingly, after dinner, Annie's mom had told Doug and Ethan that they had to leave their sister and Frankie alone for the rest of the night, and had shuffled them upstairs to watch a movie before bedtime. She'd also taken Fletch with her, leaving Frankie and Annie alone in the living room.

Knowing this was his chance, and mentally thanking Emily for allowing him to spend some time alone with Annie, Frankie turned off the overhead lights, the glow from the twinkling lights on the

Christmas tree giving the room a romantic and peaceful feeling.

He sat on the couch next to Annie, and she immediately snuggled into his side. Putting his arm around her shoulders, Frankie couldn't help but think about sometime in the future, when they'd be in their own house doing this exact thing. Maybe they'd have kids, and they'd be upstairs in their beds while he and Annie got some much-needed alone time.

He smiled, knowing he was being fanciful. They were only sixteen, they had plenty of time to settle down and have kids. Annie had a lot to accomplish in her life. College and a career in the Army. She was going to do amazing things, Frankie just knew it.

"I don't want you to go," Annie whispered.

"I know. I've loved being here with you and your family," Frankie told her.

Annie sighed and tightened her arm around his belly for a moment.

Frankie took a deep breath and said the words that had been rattling around his brain all week. "I love you, Annie Fletcher. I don't care if other people think it's too early. That we're too young. I know what I feel. From the first day we met, you accepted me as I am, a weird deaf kid who couldn't even communicate with you. We clicked that day, and every day since. I'll wait as long as it takes to make you mine. And I'll always support you no matter what it is you want to do with your life."

"Frankie," Annie whispered, sitting up and staring at him with wide eyes.

"I'm serious," he told her. "You're the best thing that's ever happened to me. I live for your phone calls, and my day isn't complete without a few dozen texts from you. I hate that we live on other sides of the country, but that hasn't—and will never—change how I feel about you. You're the other half of my soul...which is corny, but I don't care."

"Oh, Frankie. I love you too," Annie said.

Sighing in relief at hearing the words, Frankie leaned to the side and pulled the gift out of his pocket that he'd been carrying around for a week now. He had misgivings, now that the time to give it to her was here, but he swallowed down his nervousness and held out the gift on the palm of his hand.

"I didn't wrap it in fancy paper, but it's from my heart. I want to marry you someday," he said. "I want you to be Mrs. Frankie Sanders. Or Annie Sanders. Or keep your name. I don't care. All I care about is making you mine, and being yours officially in return. It doesn't matter if that happens when we're eighteen or eighty-two. I'll love you no matter what."

Annie stared at the ring in the palm of his hand, and Frankie continued speaking nervously. "This isn't an engagement ring. Your dad would have a connip-tion fit if we got engaged right now when we're only sixteen. Besides, I know he expects me to ask him for permission to marry you. That scares the shit out of me, but I'll do anything for you. But anyway, this is a promise ring. A promise from me to you. A promise that I'll never raise my hand to you in anger—you'd probably knock me on my ass if I tried." Frankie knew he was babbling, but he couldn't stop now.

"A promise I'll support you no matter what you want to do in life. When you join the Army, I'll be right there at your side even if we have to move every year to a different post. It's a promise that I'll love you no matter what. A promise that you can count on me. I love you, Annie. And it doesn't even scare me because it just feels right."

Annie hadn't moved. Not one inch. She simply stared down at his palm.

All of a sudden, Frankie was having second thoughts. He'd worked his ass off to raise enough money to get her this ring. He'd seen it in a jeweler's window back in California and knew immediately that he wanted to get it for her. It was platinum, with two oval opals set in the band. They didn't stick up and shouldn't snag on anything. He'd talked to his dad, who'd talked to Cooper, his godfather, who'd talked to his wife, who'd talked to Annie's mom in order to get the size of Annie's middle finger on her right hand.

But maybe she didn't like it? She wasn't all that interested in makeup or jewelry in general. Maybe he should've gotten her something else. His confidence wavered as she simply sat there staring at the ring.

"If you don't like it, it's okay," Frankie said hesitatingly.

"Not like it?" Annie asked. "It's the most beautiful thing I've ever seen in my life."

Frankie mentally sighed. Thank God. He reached out for her right hand and slowly slipped the ring down her middle finger. Bringing her hand up to his mouth, he kissed the ring at the base of her finger.

"It fits perfectly," she breathed. "And look," Annie said as she pretended to give someone the finger. "When I flip someone off in the future, I'll always think of you."

Frankie burst out laughing. Leave it to his Annie to think of that.

Then her face fell.

"What? What's wrong?" Frankie asked anxiously.

"My present to you seems really stupid now."

"Nothing you could ever give me could be stupid," Frankie reassured her.

"Wait until you see it before you say that," Annie muttered, standing up and going over to the

Christmas tree. She picked up a small package, brought it back to the couch, and handed it to him.

Frankie smiled at her before tearing open the wrapping.

"After what you did at the mall, I asked my mom if she would go back and pick something up that I saw when we were wandering around. It made me think of you. It doesn't compare to my ring though."

Frankie stared at the gift in his hands and a lump formed in his throat.

"It's a bobblehead," Annie said a little self-consciously.

It was. A cartoon man, with the requisite huge head that bobbed up and down on the spring inside, his hands on his hips, wearing a large red cape. On the stand, the words "My Hero" were printed.

Frankie had never been anyone's hero before. He was the poor deaf kid. The one whose mother tried to kidnap him. The boy who talked funny and who was skinny and gangly. The idea that Annie thought of him as her hero did weird things to his insides.

"Told you it was stupid," Annie muttered.

"I love it," Frankie reassured her.

She shrugged and wouldn't meet his eyes.

Frankie knew he'd think of his Annie every time he saw that bobblehead. He wanted to be her hero. Wanted her to look up to him. The fact that she'd thought of *him* when she'd seen the toy bowled him over.

He carefully placed her gift on the table next to the couch, then he took her face in his hands, waiting until she finally looked up and met his gaze. "I love you," he said softly. "You could give me a rock and I'd think it was the bestest rock in the world. But knowing you think of me that way? As your hero? I'm speechless."

They stared at each other for a long moment, then Frankie brushed his thumb back and forth over her cheek. "I want to kiss you."

"Yes. Please," Annie said.

"Our first kiss," he whispered, wanting to prolong the moment, make it last. Make this a memory they could both think about for the rest of their lives.

Annie licked her lips.

Then Frankie slowly leaned forward, not letting go of her face. He brushed his lips against hers lightly, letting her scent of peaches and strawberries fill his nostrils.

He kissed her again, lingering longer this time. Annie's eyes had closed and she held on to his shoulders.

Making a split-second decision, Frankie urged Annie to straddle his thighs. Her dad would probably have a heart attack if he walked in and saw them sitting like this, but Frankie didn't care. He needed to be closer to her. Needed to be able to kiss her without having to crane his neck and, more importantly, without Annie being the least bit uncomfortable.

"This okay?" he asked.

"Perfect," Annie reassured him, scooting closer until she could most definitely feel the erection in his pants. But for the first time in his life, Frankie wasn't embarrassed about his body's reaction. This was Annie. He had nothing to be self-conscious about with her. Now wasn't the time to make love with her. Oh, he wanted that, but he didn't want to rush her in any way. For now, kissing her would be enough.

Then Annie's head lowered, and she kissed *him*. Frankie ran his tongue over the seam of her lips, and she immediately opened for him. His heart beating out of his chest, Frankie turned his head to get a better angle and tentatively touched his tongue to hers. For a heartbeat, things felt awkward, but proving they were on the same page, the strangeness morphed into something right...for them both.

Frankie and Annie moaned at the same time— and then they were kissing as passionately as if they'd done it hundreds of times before. Their tongues intertwined as they learned each other's mouths.

How long they sat there with their lips locked

together, Frankie didn't know, but when they finally pulled apart, they were both breathing as if they'd run a hundred-meter dash.

Frankie ran a hand over her head, smoothing her hair back as he stared at her. "You are so beautiful," he said softly, licking his lips and tasting her there.

"You make me feel beautiful," Annie said. Then she leaned forward, curled her arms between them, and rested her head on his shoulder. Frankie could feel her warm breaths against his neck, and he closed his eyes in contentment.

Yeah, this was what he wanted. Who he wanted. Annie. In his arms. Soft and warm and content. Frankie wasn't an idiot; there would be hard times ahead for them both. Long-distance relationships weren't easy, but he loved Annie with all his heart. He'd make this work. No matter what it took.

"Merry Christmas, Annie," he said softly as he held her against his chest.

"Merry Christmas, Frankie."

———

Emily headed down the hallway after finally getting John to sleep. The toddler had been especially ornery tonight and it had taken all her tricks to finally get him to lie down and close his eyes. She'd checked on

Doug and Ethan and found them engrossed in the movie she'd put in for them earlier.

She was about to walk to the master bedroom to see what her husband was up to, when something caught her eye at the bottom of the stairs.

Fletch was standing there, staring into the living room.

Careful not to make a noise, Emily tiptoed down the stairs to see what her husband was looking at so intently. The lights from the Christmas tree lent an intimate glow to the living room...and their daughter and her boyfriend.

She came up beside Fletch and put her arm around his waist, leaning into him as they watched Frankie open Annie's gift. It was easy to see how affected he was by her choice.

"Told you it was stupid," they heard Annie say.

"I love it," Frankie told her.

Emily tensed as she watched her daughter shrug as if it didn't matter what Frankie thought of her gift. But she knew it did. And Frankie didn't let either of them down. He placed the bobblehead on the table next to the couch then took Annie's face in his hands.

"I love you. You could give me a rock and I'd think it was the bestest rock in the world. But knowing you think of me that way? As your hero? I'm speechless."

Emily mentally sighed. She'd always liked Frankie. He was down-to-earth and a genuinely good kid. And watching him with her daughter, she liked him even more. He treated her as Emily's own husband treated *her*. With respect. And he'd never be afraid to show her how much he loved her. What more could a mother ask for her daughter?

"I want to kiss you," Frankie told Annie.

"Yes. Please," Annie replied.

"Our first kiss," Frankie said softly, making Emily smile. Her daughter hadn't overstepped any bounds with her boyfriend the week he'd been here, and she'd trusted Frankie. Which was the only reason they'd allowed him to stay in their house. If she'd thought for one minute either Annie or Frankie would go further than was appropriate, she and Fletch wouldn't have allowed the teenager to come to Texas for the week.

As Frankie leaned toward Annie, Emily felt more than heard Fletch growl next to her. Annie might be a mature sixteen, but she was still Fletch's little girl. Still his sprite.

So she ducked under her husband's arm to stand in front of him. Planting her hands on his chest, she gave him a little push backward. She nodded with her chin toward the stairs behind them.

Fletch frowned and shook his head.

Emily glared at him and pointed at the stairs this time.

With a sigh, Fletch finally turned and silently headed up toward their room.

Looking back once more before following her husband, Emily saw Annie had straddled Frankie's lap and they were kissing once more. Smiling, loving that her daughter was learning about love with someone like Frankie, Emily followed after Fletch.

Once the door to their room was shut, Fletch immediately said, "She's too young for kissing."

Emily couldn't help it, she laughed. "When did you have your first kiss?"

Fletch frowned. "We're talking about Annie, not me."

"Right. Let me guess, you were around ten?"

"Eleven," Fletch grumbled.

Emily smiled and walked up to her husband. She didn't stop until she was plastered against him from chest to thighs. Looking up, loving how he towered over her, Emily said, "Frankie's a good kid. He'll take care of her."

Fletch sighed. "I just...it's hard to see her grow up."

"I know."

"And she's my only daughter. I want to protect her

from all the bad things in the world. If I could keep her in a bubble forever, I would."

"Annie's an incredible young woman. Smart, cautious, and she has a good head on her shoulders. We've been lucky and haven't had to deal with much of the normal teenage angst I've seen other parents go through."

"I'll never forget the panic I felt when I realized Jacks had taken both of you," Fletch said quietly. "I still see her as that little six-year-old. Scared, but telling me that her mom had said being scared just meant she was going to do something really brave."

Emily smiled. She hated that her husband still thought about that asshole Jacks, who had kidnapped her and Annie so long ago. "You've raised her to be tough, honey. You've got to let her go sometime."

"But not yet," Fletch grumbled.

"Not yet," Emily agreed. She had a feeling she needed to distract her husband before he stormed down the stairs and insisted on putting a large pillow between their daughter and her boyfriend for propriety's sake. She ran her hands up and down his chest. "John's asleep, and Doug and Ethan will be distracted by their movie for at least another hour," she said as seductively as she could.

"Yeah?" Fletch asked, the interest easy to hear in his tone.

"Yup."

"Hmmm, I think it's been too long since I've been inside my wife," Fletch said in the low, rumbly tone he used when he got turned on, which Emily loved.

She laughed. "Um...forgive me, as I'm getting old and senile, but wasn't it just last night that you made love to me so hard that I almost passed out?"

"As I said, it's been too long," Fletch said before lowering his head.

Emily sighed. This man was everything she thought didn't exist in the male species. But he'd proved time and time again that he was the kind of man women wrote romances about. Loyal, protective, supportive...and every other positive adjective she couldn't think of at the moment. Not when he was turning her on so much.

Turning them, Fletch made quick work of her shirt and bra, then shoved her leggings over her hips before throwing her backward onto their mattress. Laughing, Emily kicked both her leggings and underwear off as Fletch knelt over her. He undid the fasteners on his jeans, but didn't bother to take off his shirt or even remove his pants all the way.

Emily pouted. "I want you naked."

"I want to *be* naked," Fletch returned. "But my sixteen-year-old daughter is downstairs making out with her boyfriend, our boys could get bored with their movie any second, and our toddler is one slammed door away from waking up and crying his heart out for his mommy. Someone needs to stay mostly dressed to deal with our children and any interruptions that might happen."

Excitement rolled through Emily. "Right. Then you should get on with making love to your wife, huh?"

Fletch didn't need any other encouragement before his head dropped between her legs. He always made sure she was more than turned on and wet before entering her. It was one more thing she loved about her man.

When she was ready, Fletch came up on his knees and pushed inside her with one long, hard thrust, making them both moan softly. Then he made hard, fast love to her. She came too quickly, trembling and shaking with the intensity of her orgasm. It only took Fletch three more hard thrusts before he followed, exploding deep inside her body.

Twenty seconds later, they both heard a loud, whiny voice from down the hall. "Mooooom! Ethan is hogging the beanbag! It's my turn!"

Fletch sighed and lifted his head where he'd let it fall bonelessly against her shoulder after he came. He smiled down at her and brushed a stray lock of hair off her slightly sweaty forehead. "I'll go deal with them. You stay here. Naked and drowsy. I'm gonna want to do that again once I get the boys settled, and make sure my daughter and her boyfriend haven't gone too far."

Emily knew she should probably get up, put her clothes back on and help her husband deal with their brood, but she was too comfortable at the moment. Besides, all it would take was one stern word from Daddy, and Doug and Ethan would calm down. She was also confident that there was no way Frankie would disrespect Annie—or her and Fletch—by seducing their daughter on the couch. But that didn't mean she couldn't give him some incentive to hurry back to her.

"Okay," she said, running a hand down her naked body seductively. "I'll be right here."

"Damn, woman," Fletch complained as he refastened his pants after standing. He leaned over and kissed her long and deep before lifting his head. "I love you."

"I love you too."

"Do you remember our first kiss?" he asked out of the blue.

"Yes. Do you?"

"We were on my couch and were playing that 'get to know you' game. I'd just convinced you to live with me, and you agreed to go on a date. I was holding your hands, and I leaned over, and the second my lips touched yours, I knew my life had changed...for the better."

"Wow, you *do* remember," Emily said.

"It's seared on my brain," he admitted. "I like Frankie. He's going to be a good man. And I hope like hell he appreciates what he has in our daughter."

"He does," Emily said without hesitation.

"And I hope our daughter remembers her first kiss as fondly as I do mine, with you," Fletch said. Then he turned and headed for the door.

The second it closed behind him, Emily repositioned herself on the bed and got under the covers. She turned on her side and sighed in contentment. Her life was chaotic with four kids, and a husband who sometimes drove her crazy, but she wouldn't change one thing about it.

She was so happy that her daughter had found someone who seemed to love her as much as her own husband loved Emily. "Hang on to him, Annie," Emily whispered. "A guy who'll appreciate getting a bobblehead as a gift is a precious thing."

Closing her eyes, Emily couldn't help but wonder where her daughter's life would take her. Would she join the Army? Would she and Frankie stick it out? Would she have children?

Whatever happened, Emily knew Annie would be all right.

And now she had the memory of a perfect first kiss to look back on too.

Emily fell asleep before Fletch returned and never even felt him climbing under the covers with her. She didn't feel him kiss her forehead and hold her close. All she'd felt before drifting off was safety, and love, and the certainty that all her children were happy and healthy at the moment. All was right in their world.

Also by Susan Stoker

SEAL of Protection Series

Protecting Caroline

Protecting Alabama

Protecting Fiona

Marrying Caroline (novella)

Protecting Summer

Protecting Cheyenne

Protecting Jessyka

Protecting Julie (novella)

Protecting Melody

Protecting the Future

Protecting Kiera (novella)

Protecting Alabama's Kids (novella)

Protecting Dakota

SEAL of Protection: Legacy Series

Securing Caite

Securing Brenae (novella)

Securing Sidney

Securing Piper

Securing Zoey

Securing Avery

Securing Kalee

Securing Jane (Feb 2021)

SEAL Team Hawaii Series

Finding Elodie (Apr 2021)
Finding Lexie (Aug 2021)
Finding Kenna (Oct 2021)
Finding Monica (TBA)
Finding Carly (TBA)
Finding Ashlyn (TBA)
Finding Jodelle (TBA)

Delta Force Heroes Series

Rescuing Rayne
Rescuing Aimee (novella)
Rescuing Emily
Rescuing Harley
Marrying Emily (novella)
Rescuing Kassie
Rescuing Bryn
Rescuing Casey
Rescuing Sadie (novella)
Rescuing Wendy
Rescuing Mary
Rescuing Macie (novella)

Delta Team Two Series

Shielding Gillian
Shielding Kinley
Shielding Aspen

Shielding Jayme (novella) (Jan 2021)
Shielding Riley (Jan 2021)
Shielding Devyn (May 2021)
Shielding Ember (Sep 2021)
Shielding Sierra (TBA)

Badge of Honor: Texas Heroes Series

Justice for Mackenzie
Justice for Mickie
Justice for Corrie
Justice for Laine (novella)
Shelter for Elizabeth
Justice for Boone
Shelter for Adeline
Shelter for Sophie
Justice for Erin
Justice for Milena
Shelter for Blythe
Justice for Hope
Shelter for Quinn
Shelter for Koren
Shelter for Penelope

Ace Security Series

Claiming Grace
Claiming Alexis
Claiming Bailey

Claiming Felicity
Claiming Sarah

Mountain Mercenaries Series

Defending Allye
Defending Chloe
Defending Morgan
Defending Harlow
Defending Everly
Defending Zara
Defending Raven

Silverstone Series

Trusting Skylar (Dec 2020)
Trusting Taylor (Mar 2021)
Trusting Molly (July 2021)
Trusting Cassidy (Dec 2021)

Stand Alone

The Guardian Mist
Nature's Rift
A Princess for Cale
A Moment in Time- A Collection of Short Stories
Another Moment in Time- A Collection of Short Stories
Lambert's Lady

Special Operations Fan Fiction

http://www.AcesPress.com

Beyond Reality Series

Outback Hearts

Flaming Hearts

Frozen Hearts

Writing as Annie George:

Stepbrother Virgin (erotic novella)

ABOUT THE AUTHOR

New York Times, USA Today, and *Wall Street Journal* Bestselling Author Susan Stoker has a heart as big as the state of Texas where she lives, but this all American girl has also spent the last fourteen years living in Missouri, California, Colorado, and Indiana. She's married to a retired Army man who now gets to follow *her* around the country.

She debuted her first series in 2014 and quickly followed that up with the SEAL of Protection Series, which solidified her love of writing and creating stories readers can get lost in.

If you enjoyed this book, or any book, please consider leaving a review. It's appreciated by authors more than you'll know.

www.stokeraces.com
susan@stokeraces.com

facebook.com/authorsusanstoker

twitter.com/Susan_Stoker

instagram.com/authorsusanstoker

goodreads.com/SusanStoker

bookbub.com/authors/susan-stoker

amazon.com/author/susanstoker

Printed in Great Britain
by Amazon

82225722R00098